Zodiac Fate

Book 1

R.C. Luna

ZODIAC FATE
Warrior Shifter Series – Book One

© 2022 by R.C. Luna
First Edition: 2022
Second Edition: September 2025

Published by Lucid Publishing, LLC
Cover Design: Miblart

ISBN: 978-1-7374109-2-8

All rights reserved. No part of this publication may be reproduced, stored in a retrieval system, or transmitted in any form or by any means—electronic, mechanical, photocopying, recording, or otherwise—without the prior written permission of the author, except in the case of brief quotations used in reviews or scholarly works, as permitted by U.S. copyright law.

This is a work of fiction. Names, characters, places, organizations, and incidents are either the product of the author's imagination or are used fictitiously. Any resemblance to actual persons, living or dead, or actual events is purely coincidental.

Other Work by R.C. Luna

Welcome to Book One of the Warrior Shifter Series. You're about to step into a world of shifters, shadows, and starlit destiny.

Use the QR code below to subscribe for behind-the-scenes insights, new release updates and exclusive content that shapes this magical world If you enjoy the journey, I'd be so grateful if you left a review. It's one of the most powerful ways to help other readers find their way into the stars.

The *Warrior Shifter* series:

Zodiac Shadows (prequel)
Zodiac Fate (Book 1)
Zodiac Chaos (Book 2)
Zodiac Prison (Book 3)
Zodiac Throne (Book 4)

This is for me

I dedicate this to all the shattered pieces of my heart.
The ones I have had to glue together, over and over.
Only to shatter once again.
To the parts of me that didn't see the wickedness in others,
until it was smoldering me in its flames.
To the part of me that fought through it all and never gave up,
no matter the pain.
You are my fucking hero.
And I promise you will never be tamed.

Letter From the Author

In this book, you will meet Sasha when she's broken. She has not yet learned to face the inescapable darkness that is coming for her. She's confused and very much alone. Her journey is not an easy one to travel. She will be confronted by deeply disturbing monsters that raise questions and spark controversy. These are complex themes, for a mature audience, and they may be triggering to many. Before you question whether any of this is possible in the real world, please remember this is a work of pure fiction in an alternate reality that is not our own.

Despite any similarities or comparisons you may want to make, none of the institutions mentioned or organizations referred to in these books, exist in our world.

However, there are very real triggers in this entire series. *There are multiple depictions of physical, sexual, and psychological abuse and violence.*

There's heartache and struggle. But if you choose to go on this journey with her throughout the entire series, you will come to see how despite her troubled past, her mistakes and all of her fears, she will experience extreme growth, mastery of her emotions, control of her inner darkness and a timeless love.

Please be cautious and aware of what could be triggering for you. Enter the series only if you are ready for this expanding new world.

With all my love,
R.C. Luna

Prologue

Three years from now – Scorpio Throne Room, Xibalba

The twin gods of death watch my every move. Impassive. Cold. They've seen queens rise before. They've seen them fall. But none like me. Powerless to control me. Unable to keep me locked in their invisible chains of servitude. Of torture.

I slowly climb the steps that lead to the throne of fire, the heat from the flames gently tickling my arms. My hands are blood-soaked, but it's not my blood. This is the blood of the dead rulers of the twelve Zodiac Houses. They refused to bow. Called me unworthy. Said I was a pretender queen, a mutt born of shadows and fire.

A low chuckle leaves my throat because they thought they were immortal. Untouchable. But instead, their stories will be forgotten, and their souls will rot in the Xibalba Underworld for all eternity.

My fate was written in the stars, centuries ago.

But the stars never said how good it would feel to unleash my fury on twelve kingdoms.

My mafia past is long behind me. So are the days of being afraid of the surrounding darkness.

Now I feed off of it.

I've seen too many battles. I've bled for too many monsters. For too many creatures far worse than I could ever imagined existed, back then.

He's here too—the Dark King. Watching. Silent. Not intervening. He could've ended my wrath with a word.

But he doesn't.

Because he doesn't want to stop me.

He wants to claim me.

When the final House fell, I didn't flinch when the head hit the floor.

Burn it all.

For the ones I loved.

For the ones I lost.

And for the empire I've taken—one blood-soaked step at a time.

Chapter 1

I saw and heard very strange things before my twentieth birthday. Like a now-familiar wicked darkness that moved and shifted in corners, indefinite and undefined. It crept forward with a certain boldness, thicker and darker than ever before.

In these solemn years before my transformation, I faintly remembered a conversation with my aunt where she explained I would meet someone to help me with all this. But she died before she could tell me that the shadows would cover the walls as they slithered toward me, accompanied by a dark mist that held the creatures of the underworld within them. *They had hands with claws that reached for me!*

I saw them, demons in the corner with feverish eyes piercing into me in the night. I always felt them there, hidden, among shadows. One had a long, reptilian tail that rattled on the body of a massive alligator with a snake's head.

But there were more. Decaying bodies with black, rotted flesh and sharp, long gray teeth, bald heads and protruding bones. Some without eyes. Some without mouths. Some without ears.

The beasts of the shadows called me to them day and night. In my nightmares there would be a gate with a zodiac sign. But I always had to fight through the shadows to get to it. That's why I called these nightmares the Zodiac Shadows.

The months went by, and the heavy darkness only got stronger, with no sign of any relief. Slowly and without me knowing it, my mind began to slip from my grasp.

It got exponentially worse after I left my ex, the rising mafia king. I'd married him in a rush to get out of my parents' house, already driven half-mad by the shadows.

And not surprisingly, that didn't work out either. My pitiful life was back to where it had all begun. In my old room at my parents' house, staring at the same popcorn ceiling I had run away from.

I shuffled from the kitchen to my room whenever absolutely necessary. My hair was oily and unwashed, my clothes stained, and it seemed nothing was ever where I left it.

One day, I made the mistake of unlocking my door while my father was in the hallway. I would've avoided him, but I couldn't hear him out there. Sounds of this world were muffled by the screeching howls of another place. Another time. He grabbed me by the hair, shoved a mop and bucket into my hands, and pressed me up against the wall. My legs and body buckled as weak as a withered flower.

"I've been knocking at your door." Spittle sprayed from his mouth, and his breath reeked of stale rum. "Didn't you hear me? Clean this place up if you want to live here."

I slowly took the mop from him, nodding and not meeting his eyes.

The desperate Zodiac Shadows swirled everywhere. The demons were my company. With my head in such a state, it was hard to remember things. What was it my aunt used to say? *Oh yes. The stars write the path.*

Just as it did every night, the Shadow would swirl around me, whispering the thoughts I dared not think, filling me with the power of its fury. A power that was ripping me apart. Sleep would only make it worse. My nightmares were so real. So disturbing that I slept as little as possible.

Until I could fight it no longer. My eyelids were heavy, the day weary upon me, I couldn't stop myself this time and fell asleep.

I was dreaming again. I stood in a busy shopping area in downtown Miami. This was where Nikki and I loved to shop for new sneakers! I searched for her, my best friend since I was six. I missed her so much since she'd moved to New York. I missed her so much I wouldn't call her because she left me all alone, and I couldn't bear to hear how happy she was in her new life.

I was lost without her.

A familiar agony washed over me every time I thought about it. But when I peered into our favorite shop, there she was, checking out a new pair of shoes.

I went right up to her, as I always did, and said, "Yo, nice kicks."

She turned to me and smiled her big, beautiful smile. It was her, nose ring and all.

"Let's get a bite to eat, Nikki," I said. "I'm hungry."

Instantly, we were sitting across from each other in my favorite bodega where they served the best Colombian arepas and coffee. I looked down, and the food was already there on my plate.

I went to take a bite of the arepa but stopped before it met my mouth. My bones froze as the Shadow crept through the windows and door, its smoke curling softly with the mist and whispers that haunted its dreadful abyss.

"Nikki, Nikki! We've got to go," I yelled, but Nikki went on telling me a story I couldn't even hear—all I heard were the high-pitched whispers.

The Shadow was inches away from her, so I got up, grabbed her hand, and pulled so we could run. But she was locked in place. Frozen. She seized my arm, and I looked into her eyes. All at once they turned pale red with a bright violet ring around her pupils. I tried to shake off the haze, but it was no use.

The Zodiac Shadows had me now.

"Sit down," the not-Nikki form growled at me.

A deep knowing stirred within me, and by command, I sat. Unable to do otherwise.

The form released its control of my mind and spoke in the most pretentious voice I'd ever heard. "Listen, because we don't have much time."

I nodded and listened, the background of the café crumbling and rebuilding into a patio by a river bend, the river black and murky. I shifted my gaze to the waves of the river, stirring and brimming. Large, dark shapes the size of humans swam just beneath the surface.

"First of all, this shadow you see around you is an infection, inside your mind," the not-Nikki said. "I can't explain now, it's all too complicated for the dream state. But I am here to tell you that you need to cross the Gate, and soon.

"Unfortunately for you, your shaman has been off the grid for a while, and your shaman is the only one who can help with your induction. Simply put, you need to find your shaman and cross the Gate, or you will lose your mind." She paused for a moment, assessing me. My brows pinched as I stared at her in utter confusion, her gaze fixed on me.

"Basically, just get your shit together and figure out a way to control your mind until you find the missing shaman and we can get you into the Aries Academy. Do you understand me?"

I stared wide-eyed at the not-Nikki and nodded robotically, even though I wasn't understanding much of anything. This creature, or mist, or force of nature—whatever it was—was giving me advice? Now? After making me fucking crazy for months?

Her voice sounded centuries old, her shoulders relaxed, and her demeanor was elegant and poised, unlike the rowdy Nikki I'd always known.

"You're behind in your training, Nagual. There is normally a formal introduction to the twelve Zodiac houses by now." The form stared away as if some distant voice was calling it. It turned back to me and said, "Remember, control your mind."

Just then, the smell of bacon and eggs overwhelmed me, and I heard my name being called from somewhere far away...

Chapter 2

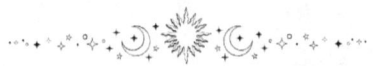

"Sasha, come to breakfast," I heard again, now clearer.

I opened my eyes and looked around. I was in bed in my old room in my parents' house. My posters and art had been removed from the walls, but the furniture remained. I was covered in sweat like I usually was after the Zodiac Shadow dreams.

But this dream had been different; the Shadow had spoken to me through Nikki. And it felt like it was trying to actually *help* me with some advice or something. My head was foggy. What was that about being behind in training? And the twelve Zodiac houses? And the Shadow-possessed-Nikki had called me "Nagual." What was a nagual?

The Shadow kept pushing in, trying to cloud my thoughts, but I knew this was important. I had to make sense of the words spoken in the dream with Nikki. I grabbed my phone and searched up nagual on the web.

Wikifacts said the nagual was part of Mesoamerican mythology, a kind of shaman, witch or mage who had the power to shapeshift into a jaguar form. They could travel between the spirit world and the physical world, and the traits of a nagual were determined by their birthdate and time.

Vague memories of conversations I'd overheard between my mother and my aunt Lily echoed in my mind. But those memories were clouded, gray and splotchy. I couldn't remember anything clearly.

So, the dream was saying I was a jaguar shapeshifter? Not a wolf, not a dragon, not a phoenix. But a jaguar? Of all the animals the stars would choose for me, I was a big cat. Well, that was kind of cool. If it was true.

I mean, Tia Lily did tell me some wild things when I was younger, and my mother always argued with her about indulging my imagination. Then there were the jaguar dreams, where I dreamed of running in the jungle with large black claws. Maybe I was still holding on to some of Lily and her wild stories, even after all this time.

I went to the kitchen. It was rare for my mother to cook breakfast. She must have been off work today. My brother was probably at football practice, so it was just my father, her and me at the table. I served myself a piece of bacon and some scrambled eggs that were in the pans on the stove.

"What's going on with you Sasha?" My mother asked me as I sat down at the table across from her.

"I got divorced yesterday," I mumbled.

"¿Aha, sí? I didn't even know you were married." She rolled her eyes and pursed her lips. "Did you hear that, Dante? Our daughter is making us so proud."

I glanced over at my father, and my heart began to race. His eyes were bloodshot-red in an extreme, odd way. I looked around for the Shadow, and there it was—a slight haze lifted from where the light wasn't hitting, in the faint shadow resting near his left arm and the back of the chair.

I raised my eyebrows and scooted back, ready to run.

"Sigue, what else is new?" Lola stayed my exit. She put her chin on her hand and eyed me again, sarcastically.

I couldn't believe she didn't see this. *How was she not afraid?*

I looked back at my father and saw he was entirely back to normal. The shadow mist had vanished. I shook my head quickly from side to side. *It must be the lack of sleep*, I thought, *and the extreme hunger.* I couldn't remember the last time I ate. I took a sip of water before answering her question.

It came back to me. Words from the dream, like a soft echo lingering in the air. Something about getting my shit together. "I'm going to join the military," I blurted out. I had been thinking about doing this, but I hadn't made a decision until just then.

"¿De verdad? Ha! You're lucky if they even let you in with your history." She let out a ridiculous laugh. "What do you think of that, Dante?" She nudged him.

He looked up at me now with the same deep green eyes I saw when I looked in the mirror every day.

With a slight furrow in his brow, he said, "Sounds great."

That was the first time he had spoken to me about anything of importance since I could remember. He'd probably just said that because he wanted me gone. His usual mood was angry-drunk, and I avoided him as much as possible. You never knew what would set him off, or when.

He had a quick temper and would lash out, landing his fists on my face at the slightest hints of sarcasm or defiance. It was no easier for Lola, my mother.

When my brother and I were little, we'd spent many nights sleeping in the car or at a shelter after he'd terrorized her. Once, it seemed he had almost killed her. But she always came back.

That's why this time I breathed a sigh of relief at his nonconfrontational comment. I nodded and ate fast, before the mist returned.

"Thank you for breakfast mami, it was delicious." I gave her a kiss on the cheek and placed the dishes in the dishwasher.

After I took a shower and got dressed I retrieved a Post-it Note from my drawer with a phone number on it. The paper had been given to me by a friend—correction, an angel—who had come into my life when I'd needed him the most, as my divorce attorney. When I was at my worst, homeless and desperate, he suggested I join the military and gave me the number of his brother, who happened to be a recruiter.

Joining the military wasn't just a chance to escape my slowly spiraling life; I was drawn to it. It probably had something to do with the fact that my zodiac sign was Aries, a fire sign ruled by Ares, the God of War.

The stars wrote the path, as my Titi Lily would say. And that day the stars spoke to me in my horoscope, and I listened.

Today you will need to make a difficult decision that will change the rest of your life. You must go toward the uncertainty, break through your comfort zone and take a chance on yourself. This is how you find exactly what you are looking for.

I dialed the number, and by some miracle he answered my call immediately. We spoke for some time about what it was like in the service, what he liked about it and how to join. I didn't waste any time. He walked me through the next steps, and within a few weeks, I would take the military entrance exam. At least now I had a plan.

I ate enough to gain back a few pounds, and my clothes fit me again.

That was when I decided to get fit. I began running a mile a day, then two miles, then three, until I was up to six miles a day. After each run, I would do a round of sit-ups and push-ups, just like the recruiter told me I would need to do in boot camp. The dark torment of the Shadow quelled when I exercised, helping me sleep more soundly. Even still, the Shadow Dreams continued.

They seemed so real, and if I told anyone what I saw I was sure they would call me crazy, and my mother probably would have me sent to a mental institution. I wanted it to stop but didn't know how. So, I kept myself busy while I waited to take the exam.

I had just gotten home from a run when my phone rang.

"Miss Sasha Moreno, please," said a man with a deep, no BS voice.

"This is her." I straightened my back. This wasn't another debt collector, I could tell.

"This is Sergeant Hernandez from the recruiter's office. We'd like to have you come in and take the entrance exam." he said. My heart just about leaped through my chest. "Can you come in tomorrow?"

"Yes. Yes, I'll be there."

"Great, see you at zero eight hundred."

"Yes, see you then." I was supposed to work, but whatever. I would call in sick. This was my chance.

Chapter 3

I took the exam and waited. An hour passed before the broad-shouldered, six-foot sergeant with the smiling eyes called me over. With his paperwork now in front of him, he jumped right into it, explaining something about my scores being really good.

"So how did you get such a good score?" he asked, reviewing my file online. "I mean, your high school transcripts paint a completely different picture."

"Yes, well, I had a hard time in high school, but that doesn't mean I didn't learn anything."

He examined me. I exhaled. He shuffled some papers around and then crossed his arms in front of him. "Because of your high score, you have some more choices when it comes to the career detail available to you. Each career has a different start date."

"I want the soonest start date."

"Well, aren't we in a hurry." He typed something into the computer, took a moment to scan the screen in front of him, then went on to ask me a series of physical fitness questions.

"Ok. After you're done with me, you'll head back to do some mental and physical screening with the others. But for now, I still have some questions. I see from your application you speak Spanish?"

"Sí, señor."

"Here's the deal. Since you're eager to start, there's an opening for a SERE specialist that begins in a month. This is a career detail that's hard to fill because it's very physically intensive, requires a higher-than-average test score like yours," his voice trailed off as he glanced back at his screen. "They show right now that they need a Spanish speaker." His gaze met mine again. "From what you explained, you meet the physical requirements. But are you up for it?"

Seer? I thought those were prophetic types. Who knew the military needed them? Whatever. If being a seer meant I could get out of here sooner, then yes, of course I was ready. I was already seeing things anyway.

"I'm more than up for it."

"You don't know what they do yet."

"Oh yeah, good point. What's a seer?"

"It's a Survival, Evasion, Resistance, and Escape specialist. You'll train others on how to survive and escape in the most hostile and remote environments. Which means first you'll need to learn how to survive and escape." He turned his monitor to me and pointed at the description on his computer.

"Oh, now I get it, it's spelled S-E-R-E but sounds like seer. That's interesting." I'd never considered myself a survivor.

"You'll also need a secret security clearance. We can have that done in the next few weeks as long as you haven't killed anybody." He laughed, but I didn't.

Beads of sweat formed on my brow. Would I be granted a clearance with all my past run-ins with the law or with my ex being in the cartel? I shifted in my chair. I looked down at my hands, wringing them together. I just had to think.

I wanted to run out of the room and disappear. I didn't want to lie to him, but I didn't want to stay.

Cabrón. No way they're going to let me join the service. What was I even thinking? No one's going to accept me, broken as I am.

I evaluated the sergeant. So far, he seemed to think I had what it took to join. I stood up and started pacing, dark clouds filling my thoughts. *No, who was I kidding?* It was time to go. I reached for the door, ready to run.

The sergeant stopped typing and said, "Hey, hey, recruit, where are you going?"

With my hand resting on the door handle, I planted my feet in place. He'd just called me a recruit. That's what someone who had already been accepted was called. I turned around and walked back toward him. "I don't know. I panicked.

I'm sorry." *Don't lie.* "I got in some trouble over the past few years. I don't think I'll get that clearance."

"What kind of trouble?"

I gave him the short version of my ex, the rising mafia-king, a past marijuana arrest and shoplifting run-ins. He didn't even flinch. I thought he would tell me I had to leave right then and there.

"That doesn't sound too bad. Tell me, what's your ex's name?"

I fidgeted with my fingers. Should I tell him? I mean, would it come back to haunt me later? "Omar Garcia," I blurted out before I could talk myself out of it.

He turned back to his computer and did some more typing. "From what I can see, your record is clean," he said. "That's normal when you don't commit a felony, charges are filed as a minor, and you comply with all the court's requirements. As for everything with your ex, you didn't get arrested and were not implicated in any of his charges.

"Go ahead and file your clearance paperwork and everything else. Let them decide. To be honest, Sasha, I don't think you have anything to worry about. When it comes to these clearances, we're looking for threats of espionage, drug abuse, sexual misconduct and indications of certain types of psychological conditions. I'm sure you'll be fine."

I straightened in my chair.

"It's worth a try. And if you don't pass the clearance, there are still career details you could enter easily. So don't give up on yourself so quickly," he said with an easy smile. "If you keep using the same survival skills that brought you in here, you'll do great in the field. I think you've got some real potential."

I couldn't believe my ears. No one had ever told me I had potential. Would he think the same if he knew I suffered from horrific nightmares and hallucinations? Probably not, so I considered my next words carefully.

"Ok then. Let's do this."

I finally had a real chance to make something out of my life. I was going to take it.

"Great. Get your things ready, because your enlistment date is August first."

For the month that followed, becoming a SERE was all I could think about. I exercised almost every day to surpass the physical requirements, and whenever I could, I took the bus to the beach to swim. My appetite grew, and all the money I earned at the salon was spent on food.

The dreams continued, becoming a nagging companion. A constant headache, piercing the left side of my brain, then the right. During my waking hours, misty shadows appeared and disappeared on certain people, but not on others. In certain places, but not in others. Whenever I saw them, I wanted to run away. To hide.

Shit. What if I lost it while I was in boot camp? I guessed it couldn't be worse than losing it here at home. I figured that at least if I was enlisted, I would be trying.

Then the day came when I packed a small bag with essentials. As I was in my room, zipping up the bag, my mother walked in.

"Be safe. Don't get into any more trouble. And don't come to me to help you clean up something if it turns into another mess." She placed her hands on her hips, her face deadpanned.

"I know, don't worry. I won't be your problem anymore. Plus, the recruiter told me I had potential, and I believe him," I grunted.

She simply shrugged her shoulders then she placed her arms around me for a hug. "Good luck, Estrellita."

After a few seconds, I raised my arms to join the embrace for a fleeting moment and then let go. Being comforted was too close to being pitied, and I couldn't go off into this unknown new world pitying myself. Not now.

"Ok, well, I'm leaving." My heart raced. This was really it.

She walked me to the door. "Want me to drop you off? I have time."

"No, it's ok. I'll take the bus," I insisted.

I had to leave no chance for a long goodbye or a change of heart. I had to stay focused.

Just then, behind my mother, I saw the dark mist lurking in the corner of the room. It pulsed and thrummed just there, rising and falling, as though it was breathing. My eyes locked on the shadowy expanse as I heard it call to me.

Sasha.

I stared into the deep, endless black haze. So dark no light could exist in it. Only a pulsing, curling and drifting depth.

"Sasha?" My mother said and I snapped my eyes to her. I flung my bag over my shoulder and hurried out the door. And I didn't look back.

Chapter 4

On the way to boot camp I had a lot of time to think. I thought a lot about my Titi Lily. She tried to tell me about how I was different from other kids all those years ago, before she died. Before my world went from bright and full of potential to a hot mess.

My life was a series of mistakes. I made the mistake of working with the mafia and messing up a big job. Of marrying the wrong man at just nineteen, then divorcing him three short months later. I made the mistake of dropping out of college and ruining my chances for a good career. And I made the mistake of killing my aunt when I was just ten years old by telling her to get on the wrong plane. I lived with that guilt every day of my life, so much so that I felt it tearing me apart from the inside out.

She was the one that told me I had a very specific destiny. One that was written in the stars. What she didn't tell me was that my fate came at a cost and I paid the biggest price of all when she died.

TEN YEARS EARLIER

"And what about this, what are these colors here?" my aunt Lily said, then she pointed to the yellow-orange glow around her.

"That's your light. It's my favorite color, and your light shines brighter than any I've ever seen."

We were sitting on the couch in her living room. Lily was my mother's sister, and my family was visiting her farm in Puerto Rico for the summer. She was asking me about all the drawings I kept in my sketchbook. As soon as I told her about her special light, she wrapped both arms around me and gave me a huge hug. I loved my aunt Lily so much.

"Can I have this drawing?" she asked. "I want to frame it and put it on the wall so I can look at it every day."

My chest puffed up with pride. "Of course, I would love that."

That night, as the coquis sang in the tropical canopy surrounding us, I overheard my mother and Lily talking about my drawings. They sat outside on the porch, taking in the cool Caribbean breeze floating up from the lake nestled in the valley below the house.

"Let me keep her here in Villalba, Lola. I'll prepare her for her induction the right way. She will be summoned at the alignment, and you are just doing her more harm by ignoring it," Lily told my mother, her voice sharp and pointy, not the soft, round voice I was used to.

"Summoned? You think she will be summoned? No... not if I have anything to do with it. And no, I am not giving you my daughter." Lola took a long drink from her wine glass as she glared at Lily.

"Do you want her to end up like Celeste? Do you think that's any kind of life? It's better than the alternative, and you know it!" Lily's voice was even sharper now and cut right through the breeze.

"Why do you think I moved to Miami? To get away from you and this crazy brujeria. She isn't a descendant, she isn't a nagual, she isn't any of these ridiculous things you and the rest of your 'coven' think she is." She took in a deep breath. "If Dante hears us talking about this, he will leave me. Do you realize that?" Lola's voice was soft now.

My aunt softened her glare, and her shoulders dropped at her sister's words.

"Don't worry, we still have time." Lily smiled at her. My aunt was the older sister and had become the matriarch of the family when my grandmother died. She loved my mother very much, both as a sister and a daughter.

I didn't understand what they were talking about in the slightest. I was just a ten-year-old kid who still had imaginary friends and saw different-colored lights glowing around everyone. I also saw scary, dark monster clouds on certain people, like my dad, and in the dark corners and crevices of the world. The kids in class called me weird, and it was hard to make friends because of it. My mother hated my drawings and told me to stop talking about the lights.

But no matter what I tried, I couldn't stop seeing the lights, and I couldn't just make my dreams about them go away. At the end of the summer, when we got back to Miami, I did try. I drew unicorns and rainbows, just like my friends at school. One day, I brought home a picture of our family, with no balls of light, and she said with a huge smile, "That's beautiful, my love."

A few more months passed, and my aunt Lily came from Puerto Rico to visit us. I overheard another one of those talks with my mom about a summoning, and, when I asked my mother about it, she told me I shouldn't be sneaking around eavesdropping.

One day, my aunt took me shopping and bought me a yellow flower dress. Then she took me for ice cream. When we were sitting at the table enjoying our favorite kind, chocolate with sprinkles, she asked me with a smile, "Mija, do you still see those lights everywhere?" Her hair was a wavy golden-brown, and she had the prettiest almond-shaped eyes that always filled me with love.

"Not as much as I used to, Titi. Only sometimes now, like when I'm with you," I said.

Green and golden colors danced faintly around Lily, they made me smile in wonder. She wrapped her warm arm around me and squeezed tight. I loved it when she did that. "Estrellita, you are special, you know that, right?"

I nodded; she'd told me so plenty of times since I was a baby.

"Good. There will come a time when you will be called into service. That will be around your twentieth birthday, during the Transit of the Twelfth House."

"What does that mean?" I asked, eyes wide.

"Well, you remember your natal chart, right? We went over it at my house. When your Transitioning Mars Trine Natal Pluto is in the Twelfth House, you will be urged to act upon your deepest desires and deliver on the karma of your Soul Contract. You can't do this alone, so I will introduce you to another special person called a shaman. He will come to bring you to a school where the things that make you different—like the lights only you can see—are considered normal. And there will be others who are a lot like you. Would you like that?"

I nodded excitedly. How great would it be to meet other kids like me!

"I will be right by your side when that happens. Every time we are together, I will show you things that will help you get ready when it's your time." Her eyes searched mine. "Until then, just keep the lights you see between us, ok? Don't talk to other people about it. Not even your mother. She won't understand." Her expression darkened, and her mouth pressed into a thin line.

"But why am I special, Titi? Why is it I can see these things that others can't?" I didn't want to be different than the other kids.

"Well, it has something to do with the time and place you were born, and the fact that you are the descendant of someone like you."

I understood exactly what she meant.

"So, you mean, how I was born with the sun in the first house of Aries? And how my great grandmother was a mage from across the Gates?"

A bright, easy laugh left her throat, and I couldn't help but return the smile. "I'm glad you're keeping up with your zodiac studies. That will help you a lot." She took a bite of her own ice cream. "The stars write the path. Always remember that." She smiled and rubbed my back gently.

"Ok, I will remember, Titi." I was too concerned about the taste of the chocolate ice cream to ask any more questions. I simply nodded my head and stuffed another sweet spoonful in my mouth.

But that night I had the worst dream ever...

I was watching TV in my living room, and I saw an airplane flying over the ocean. My heart started beating fast when I watched as lightning struck the wing of the plane and black smoke came from the engine. Eyes wide, I walked closer to the TV and placed my hands on the thick glass screen.

This was aunt Lily's airplane! It was surrounded by a black monster cloud.

I could now see inside the plane, and when I did, I saw Lily as she sat in her seat with a panicked look on her face. She looked around anxiously as she heard the screams all around her. The plane shook as it shot straight down out of the air, and loud bangs sounded outside.

Purses, bags, magazines and cups shot up and around them. She seemed so scared. As the plane came even closer to crashing into the ocean, I saw her mouth move, and even though I couldn't hear what she said, I didn't see any more fear in her eyes as she whispered words to herself. Instead, she looked peaceful.

I woke up with hot tears spilling down my cheeks. I ran to my mother's room and begged her not to let aunt Lily get on the plane the next day.

All she said was, "Go back to bed, Sasha. Everything will be fine."

I went back to my room and sat at my desk. I knew my mother didn't want to see any more drawings, but right then I didn't care. I grabbed a blank piece of paper and moved aside my dolls and toys to make room to draw something that would make her pay attention. I drew an airplane facing down into the ocean with black and gray lines swirling around it.

In the morning, I showed my drawing to Lily while she was eating breakfast. Her face grew serious.

"It's ok," she said in a calm, soothing voice. "Everything will be fine."

My mother, seated next to Lily, snatched up the drawing and crumpled it into a ball. "I told you not to draw these anymore. You are scaring everyone with this craziness. It stops now."

Why wouldn't she listen?

"But she can't get on that plane, Mami! She will die," I yelled. I had never, ever yelled at Mami before.

"Sasha, that is enough. Now apologize to your Titi," she said, standing up from her chair as her eyes shot stones at me.

I looked at aunt Lily and could tell from her expression she wasn't mad at me. "I'm sorry."

Lily gave me a quick wink while my mother was still looking at me, and as my mother turned away, I hid a smile. I knew my aunt would listen. I knew she wouldn't get on that plane, not after what I'd shown her.

Later that night she came to my room. She sat on my bed and pulled me close. "I believe you, and will change my flight to a different one."

"No, don't go at all. Just stay here, Titi," I cried, wrapping my arms around her. No one understood me like she did. I didn't want her to go.

"I have to get home. Tio William's mother is sick, and we need to take care of her. But don't worry, I won't take the same flight. I promise." Her eyes were warm and comforting.

They left for the airport while I was at school the next day. Later, the phone rang as we were having dinner. I jumped in my chair. I had been nervous all evening, wondering what would happen to Titi.

My mother got up from the table and grabbed her phone from the counter. "Hello?" I locked my gaze on her. "Yes, I am Lola Rivera." Like most Hispanic women, she had kept her father's surname.

A moment later she stood completely still. I watched as all the color drained from her face. She turned to look at me, and her eyes narrowed into a look of disbelief and disgust.

Then she turned her back to me and leaned her shoulder against the wall. All her weight became too heavy for her legs, and she slumped to the ground with a heavy thud.

My father jumped up from the table and hurried over to her. He put his arm around her back, and when she looked up at him, she grasped at his collar, and all I heard was the sound of her gulping for air in between tears.

"What happened?" my father demanded as he held her close.

"It's Lily... Her plane went down in the Atlantic," she whispered.

Even though I knew this would happen, I hoped I was wrong. But more than that, I'd prayed to God I was wrong. Aunt Lily was dead because nobody listened to a ten-year-old. Especially a ten-year-old who dreamed of things before they happened and saw all kinds of strange lights surrounding other people.

Now that Titi Lily was dead, I hated my drawings.

I hated my dreams.

I just wanted to be like everyone else.

Chapter 5

"There she is, our beauty queen. I didn't know they let sorority girls into boot camp," belted out my military training instructor as I ran past him during our morning run. What that TI didn't know was how far I was from being a sorority girl or beauty queen.

It was my second week of boot camp, and our TIs were constantly barking orders and humiliating us. The recruiters explained it as resiliency training, mental conditioning and a way of teaching us to respect our superiors. I just tried to picture myself in a *Resident Evil* training camp before going after the zombies.

I was relieved my TI thought I looked like one of those girls who would even join a sorority. Even though I never saw myself in that way, it sounded good at the time. Especially since I had caught the eye of one TI in particular, TI Grange.

He was what they meant when they said there was nothing hotter than a stupidly gorgeous man in uniform. *Diablo*, the way those fatigues hugged his toned shoulders, fit across his ripped chest and strained his glutes—it took serious effort for me to stop looking at him. In fact, it was as though I couldn't help myself. I wasn't usually like this. I mean, I saw lots of hot guys in Miami. But with him, it was different. He was extremely distracting.

I don't think I had ever seen a man that attractive in my life, and being anywhere near him made joining the service entirely worth it.

We were just returning from our morning PT, and the day's exercise was particularly grueling in the forty-degree rain pounding down on us from the heavens. My squadron was resilient, and we pushed through without so much as a grunt. We learned quickly not to moan, grunt or complain during the rigorous drills. As we climbed up the staircase, we were all eager to get inside, take the cold, wet clothes off and wash up in a two-minute shower. Hurrying, we rushed up the steps side by side and bottlenecked at the entrance.

TI Grange yelled, "Make a hole!" and we clambered to stand at attention, opening a space for the TI to pass through as we lined up with our backs against the walls. It took a moment for everyone to shuffle into place, and when we did, all was silent.

Grange commanded, "Attention," then approached us one by one, his piercing eyes searching for the slightest emotion in our faces.

When he reached me, he stared for what felt like forever, and I had a chance to soak him in. His eyes, nose and mouth were perfectly placed on his face, and my cheeks flushed warm when he focused his attention on me. Ever since I'd first seen him, I couldn't stop staring. It was as though every part of me had an uncontrollable desire—for him. I had competition, though. In this past week alone, he was all these girls would talk about. I heard them wonder if he was married, they compared notes on the size of his hands and feet and they sent him flirty glances at every chance.

But now, as he came closer and stood in front of me, heated energy shot through my body and triggered all of my senses. My lips parted ever so slightly as my mind tried to picture him without his uniform on with his bare chest exposed, just for me.

My face flushed as warmth coursed through my center up into my cheeks. *Was that lust in his eyes?*

His expression darkened in that controlled, commanding way he had, and all it did was make me want him more. But then I saw a hint of fire in him. The tiny spark snapped me out of my aroused state. A vein in his neck was pulsing unnaturally.

No, I told myself, I'm just seeing things. He was close enough for my lungs to fill with the scent of orange and spice from the light cologne resting on his deep olive skin. Goosebumps lined my arms, and my core pulsed fiercely with an urge to press my lips against his.

The recruit next to me nudged me with her elbow. I'd been staring at his lips for far too long as I'd imagined them covering every part of my body.

I blinked several times. Focus. When my mind came back to me, I avoided looking into his eyes and tried to focus on something else. A dark, transparent mist lifted from his arms and chest. From the corner of my eye, I could see the swirling chaos within the shadow he cast on the floor, opening an endless abyss to an even deeper realm that existed within. I realized then, he had the all-too-familiar black monster cloud.

He must have caught a hint of my fear, because he laughed and said, "Now, would you look at that? This one's got crazy in her eyes."

Damn, even his laugh was sexy.

I squeezed my eyes shut and put my head down.

"You must be crazy because I didn't say 'at ease.' Now, you've got to get it together."

I returned my gaze to meet his and watched as he gave a captivating smile and looked around the stairwell. His smile tugged at my center. I lifted my chin and arched my back ever so slightly.

"Ok, I'll cut you some slack. Maybe you aren't crazy. Maybe you're just hungry. To be honest, sometimes I get a little crazy when I'm hungry. In fact, let me find out." He turned back to me and asked, "Are you hungry?"

What was coming over me? I couldn't throw myself at Grange. Not here, not in front of everyone. I avoided looking him in the eye and answered, "No, sir."

"Well, that's the wrong answer, Moreno. Very much the wrong answer. In fact, you should be awfully hungry considering the amount of exercise and energy you exert here in basic training." He turned to the person next to me and asked her, "I bet you're hungry, aren't you?"

"Yes, sir," she said.

"That's more like it. Honesty. Integrity. That is what we stand for." He faced me. "Now, I want you to go in, take a shower and get dressed. All by yourself. Then head over to the chow hall and get some breakfast. While you do, the rest of your squadron will be here waiting for you. Standing exactly where they are."

I took in his sharp jawline and lips, the perfect complements to his muscular chest and arms. It was strange. One minute I imagined my legs wrapped around his naked, chiseled body, and the next, I felt a deep sense of foreboding. It must be my clouded mind.

Focus, dammit. I shook my head and said, "I can't do that, sir. It's not fair to them."

"It's an order. Do it now."

"Yes, sir," I answered.

With my eyebrows raised I looked around at the other women. I hated doing this to them, but I knew I had to pull myself away from this raging-hot man in front of me. I squeezed past him, feeling his stare and hot breath on my neck as I made my way around him in the tight stairwell.

Rushing, I jumped in the cold water, rinsed, brushed my teeth and combed my now short hair that fell right above my collar. I quickly put on my camouflage uniform and stormed off to the dining hall, passing all the girls still standing in the stairway. Their icy stares cut through me as I walked by.

In the dining hall, I picked up one hardboiled egg, a piece of toast and a half cup of water. I ate in less than two minutes and was about to stand when the TI approached with a heaping plate of food.

"Now, Moreno, that's not a healthy breakfast. Here, have this." He set the plate in front of me. "After you eat every bite, you can head back to the dorm. And don't forget your electrolytes. You need your strength, beauty queen."

The plate was filled with a stack of three pancakes, three scrambled eggs with cheese, a fruit cup, two slices of bacon and three glasses of yellow, blue, and orange liquid. It was more than I ate in a whole day, let alone at breakfast.

My shoulders slumped for a moment, but I resolved to finish it. I dug my fork in and got to work stuffing my face. After about five minutes, I was shoving the last bites of food in my mouth.

In short, efficient movements, I headed back to the dorm. People moved around me as other squads headed to the cafeteria, lining hallways and dormitories. I kept a fast pace as I made the short trek back to our dorm. When I arrived, Grange was already there.

He yelled, "At ease," and instantly the girls breathed a huge sigh of relief and hurried to prepare themselves for breakfast. Two passing me on their way to the bathroom shoved me with their shoulders and gave me dirty stares. I didn't blame them. I would hate me, too.

The squadron, now cleaned up and in their cammies, were lined up and ready to leave for breakfast when Grange shouted, "Everyone can go to breakfast. Except Moreno. Since you already ate, stay behind. I think you can help your fellow recruits get a head start on inspection by cleaning the showers."

"Yes, sir."

Ok, so I didn't hate the idea of being alone with him, at all.

Chapter 6

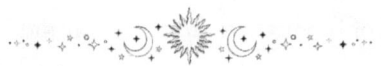

The silence they left behind in the dorm was quickly filled with the high-pitched whispers from the Shadow that drew upon Grange's presence.

Why now? I resisted the urge to look around at the darkness I could feel creeping in from every corner of the room, every place the light didn't hit.

Grange approached me as I stood at attention at the foot of my bed. First of all, was he bringing this creepy, dark shadow mist on? Second of all, what was coming over me that had me wanting him to rip my clothes off?

He stood directly in front of me, and it took all of my self-control to keep myself from biting my lip and batting my eyes.

"How was breakfast? You really need to eat more." He looked me up and down. "What do you weigh, a hundred pounds? The physical activity here is intense, and you'll need your energy."

He... noticed me? Heat rose to my cheeks. "Thanks, sir. I'll be sure to eat more."

"Now, tell me," he said, taking a step closer. "What is a pretty girl like you doing in a place like this?"

I avoided looking at him because of my raging hormones. He grabbed my chin in his hand and turned my face toward him. I looked directly at his shoulders then because he stood a whole head taller than me. He pulled my chin up with his hand and forced me to look into his rich, black eyes.

My body thrummed with desire, and the longer I looked at him, the harder it was to resist. He lowered his face to meet my lips, and the connection made my blood heat. I felt his tongue melt inside my mouth, and I leaned into him. I reached my hands up and clung to the creases of his uniform.

He pulled away, and my breath came in rapid pants. I found it hard to fill my lungs with air as my body surged with the excitement of his touch.

"You look like a nice girl, Moreno, but I think you're hiding something. You don't have a whole lot of friends here. You certainly didn't make any today."

My hands still clung to his uniform, tugging at him. I tried to pull him closer, but he didn't budge.

"Your training is only going to get harder, not easier. Do you want these girls to hate you?" he asked in a low voice.

"No, sir," I answered.

I couldn't go crazy. Fuck that. And what was up with those strange sparks in his eyes? Now that was not normal, or I was already batshit crazy.

I took a look at my hands and breathed in his spicy scent. All I wanted to do right then was unbutton his shirt and caress that perfectly muscular chest I knew lay just underneath his uniform. The mist clinging to him stopped me from doing just that when it shot an ice through my bones.

"Then you're going to have to let me help you." Grange placed his hand back on my chin and stared down at me, his eyes dropping to my lips and lingering there for several heartbeats. "If you play your cards right, I won't tell anyone I found this knife in your personal belongings. This will get you kicked out of here in a second." A small pocketknife instantly appeared between his fingers, and he twirled it around.

"That's not mine, sir." I yanked my face out of his grip. A fire rose in my chest as I realized he was toying with me. The tips of my fingers scorched hot, and I felt their heat sting my flesh.

"Well, between me and you, I also heard you made a pass at one of the other girls in the shower yesterday. This isn't looking good for you." The side of his lips curled up into the faintest smile while the mist loomed around him.

My eyes widened with shock. What in the actual *fuck* was he talking about?

I almost broke my stance but quickly pulled myself back together. He wanted something. I softened my expression; I also wanted something. My entire body felt electric the closer he came to me. He was standing only six inches away, so close I could reach my arms around him and feel the pressure of his hard body against mine. I was ready to convince him he was confused about the knife. It must have been put there by one of the other girls.

"I might just cover for you," he said. "After all, you are new to this way of life. Some things can be overlooked. But I'll need you to do something for me."

The back of his hand grazed my chest, and my flesh quivered at his touch. *I would do anything for you.* I felt the warmth of his hand as he placed it on my side, and when he tightened his grip, he pulled me in closer. His other hand reached up to my neck, and he tilted my head to the side, his hot breath making my neck tingle in all the right ways.

Where his mouth met my skin, I felt a sharp, piercing pain and let out a yell that unintentionally came out muffled and soft. Goose bumps prickled all over my flesh, and I felt a deep pull from within the skin of my neck.

I tried to push against his hard, firm chest, but it was as though I had no strength at all. My mind wandered, drifted away somewhere blurry where I couldn't see any light.

"You are mine now. I *own* you," he said, his voice deep and guttural.

He released my neck from his teeth, and I staggered backward. When I heard his voice, my mind came back to me, and I regained some control of my legs. I was able to think again, as though I had been in a deep sleep and had just woken up.

What was happening? Oh yes, I was here in the military dorms. I was listening to Grange. He was giving me an order, his commands making my insides grow warm. Throbbing.

I looked up into his black eyes. They glowed with red sparks. *He is so hot*, I thought at first. In fact, that thought was on repeat in my mind.

Then I saw the mist again, swirling around his hands, arms and head. That was when I realized he was something wicked.

As much as I wanted him, a quiet voice inside me was trying to warn me. My mind wasn't clear around him. But even as this nagging intuition pulled at me, I couldn't go against him right now. Because if I did, I could get myself kicked out of here.

Shit. My body was aching for him, and I couldn't stop myself from doing what he wanted me to do. Plus, I couldn't go back to that miserable place called home.

I pulled off my shirt and let him take me in.

He reached for my breasts and gripped one in his hand. I let out a soft moan of excitement as my hands reached up to unbutton his uniform. As soon as I caught a glimpse of his muscular chest, I lunged so my lips could meet his flesh. The taste of him was pure ecstasy, and it only rose in me a frantic need to feel his hands all over my body.

Grange pressed his fingers into my sides as he pulled me closer to him, inching a hand lower until he rested it just on top of the waist of my pants. A warm, pulsing heat grew from my center. He moved my head to the side and that piercing, sharp pain bit through my skin once again. His low growl reverberated through my veins.

I fisted the fabric of his pants as I began to black out again. Just then, he jerked his head back quickly and told me to get dressed. My vision was all hazy, and I couldn't make sense of what he was saying, but he was pulling on his shirt really fast and telling me to zip up my pants.

After I was done getting dressed, we heard people moving up the stairwell.

"How did you know?" I wondered out loud as he took several steps back from me.

"Vampire ears."

I chuckled because surely it must've been a joke. This was all so funny, and my body was still warm from his touch.

The sides of his mouth curled up into a wily smile, and I remembered the feel of his lips on my neck. He placed his divine hands where he had bitten me and applied pressure for five long seconds. "We'll continue this later."

My heartbeat pounded in my ears as I let out a long, shaky breath. Two TIs came in, and I dropped to my knees, tucking in the bedsheets at the side of my bed.

"Sergeant Grange, we need to coordinate today's drill. We've got to cover for Sergeant Smith," said one of the TIs.

"Right. Maternity leave." His eyes were hooded when he glanced back at me. "All right, let's discuss this in my office."

The men retreated to Grange's office, and the darkness that had filled the room with howls and whispers followed him. Still, I was dazed and a bit confused, but I wondered, why would it follow him and not stay here to torture me?

As soon as he left, a silent tear fell from my eye, burning my cheek as it went. I wanted to scream, to tell someone how confused I was, but no one would understand. In fact, I didn't understand. I might have even imagined it all. After all, I was seeing things now—very scary things—all day, everywhere.

Here, among so many strangers, it was getting harder to cope with the burden of the darkness tormenting me. When I looked in the mirror, my forehead had a crease in the middle, and my black hair needed brushing. I felt a soreness in my neck and rubbed it, but there was nothing there. He'd bitten me there, hadn't he? I couldn't remember; it was hazy.

It occurred to me that I could be full-blown crazy, like schizophrenic or something. I had been hallucinating for some time, and clearly my hallucinations were getting worse. A soft echo resounded in my ears, and I faintly remembered the message of one of my dreams. I tried to remember. It came through clearer now. *Cross the Gate, or you will lose your mind.*

I stood up from the side of the bed and reached into my pocket to grab my tiny book of Psalms. I couldn't get myself into any make-believe academy. I needed some mysterious missing shaman to do that. The one thing I could do was fight against losing my mind. I held the tiny book in my hand and said a silent prayer for my sanity before joining the others at formation.

As we continued with our day, TI Grange's shadow became something of a fascination. I counted our footsteps as we marched from the dorm to combat arms training to keep my feral thoughts at bay. As we stepped in unison under the bright sun, I watched his dark companion bend and weave on the ground while I heard the almost-incomprehensible whispers emitting from its center.

Averting my eyes, I focused on the back of the head of the person in front of me. Whew, no shadow. Not even a glimmer. Weird because I imagined I saw it everywhere at this point. Ok, I told myself, just focus on this person. Yes, that was a good idea. If I could just focus on this one Shadow-free person, maybe it would be my safe place during the day.

When we got to weapons training, I made sure to sit at the table behind her. This way, I could keep staring at the back of her head if I needed to. When we were in position with our guns in front of us, I looked up at her again. Not only did she not have the Shadow—now she was positively glowing. Damn it! What now?

I looked around the room; a lot of the girls were glowing. The whispery mist had quieted in my ears as the number of glowing women increased. Their energy felt positive and light.

My heartbeat slowed. I could breathe again after the morning's adrenaline rush and was finally able to concentrate on checking, loading and unloading the weapon. I did it repeatedly until I felt the woman I was staring at earlier turn around and watch me.

"You're fast," she said in an adorable Southern twang.

I returned the smile. "Thank you. Can't wait to get out and start shooting."

I stayed close to her during the entire shooting practice.

"You're a natural," she said after watching me shoot all sixteen rounds precisely. "How did you get so good?"

"Oh, probably just lucky shots today," I said. I almost told her how I did it, but figured it was too much detail.

I counted the seconds it took me to get in position (twenty-five), the seconds it took me to aim (six), and the seconds it took to pull the trigger (three). Then the seconds it took to aim and shoot again (six). I did this every time, and every time I tried to improve my time. Focusing on the tiniest detail of any task in front of me was the only way to keep thoughts of anything else out, like the Zodiac Shadows.

TI Grange came by to review our targets. When he got to mine, his lips curled. "I didn't know they had target practice at beauty pageants. That's quite impressive." He hovered over me as I remained in a crouched position, holding my rifle. Leaning down, he whispered in my ear, "Can't wait to see what else you can do with a gun."

Chapter 7

My entire body responded to his voice, and even the tiniest bit of attention he gave me flooded me with wanting. I was positively swooning over him, and I didn't like it. Only when I looked over at him did I see the Shadow form around him, and I fought to stifle a scream.

Again, I averted my eyes. I didn't want to give away my madness and the complete paradox of my emotions. The sight of that thing freaked me out to the same degree that I found him irresistible. Instinctively, I looked toward my new friend and caught a glimpse of the name written on her camo shirt. It read Cook.

The fact that the shadow didn't surround her offered me some glimmer of hope that it didn't contaminate every single space on this planet. Yes, she was still Shadow-free. She looked back at me and then down at her rifle.

"What's going on, recruit? Look at me when I'm talking to you," TI Grange snarled.

All the other recruits hung on his every word, and even though my insides throbbed with heat as he approached, I was deathly afraid of his shadow.

"Yes, sir." I unwillingly looked up at him again and told myself to count the seconds until he was gone.

"You taste incredible," he whispered in a voice only I could hear, and licked his lips. "I am coming back for seconds."

Again, my body betrayed me by going limp at the sound of his voice, and the unwanted feeling in between my thighs increased.

He pivoted on his heel and walked away in ten seconds, ignoring me completely as he tormented the other recruits. The dark Shadow released the grip around my throat as he left. I was a walking contradiction of sensations.

"You have definitely caught his attention." Cook said with a playful smile. "The other girls are probably jealous. I know I am."

She stared after him, raking her eyes up and down his body as he walked away.

I looked up toward the clear blue sky and then back down at my gun, very confused. "The malicious have a dark happiness. I try to remember that whenever I meet people like him," I grunted, more to myself than to her. She obviously didn't see what I saw.

"Oh, yeah. That man is tall, dark, and savage, and it makes me very happy." She laughed.

"You know, you remind me of my best friend from back home. Nikki."

It'd been so long since I'd thought of her. The tightness returned to my throat as memories of her washed over me. Then Titi Lily's face flashed in my mind, surrounded by a bright yellow-and-orange glow.

"What, is she dead?" Cook asked. "You should see the look on your face."

"Oh, no. No, she's not dead." I shook it off and smiled. "I just haven't spoken to her in a while. I really miss her."

"Then you should call her when we get the next patio break," she said, giving me a quick smile.

I wished I could tell her the truth about what I saw, or how I felt, but she would just think I was crazy. Heck, I thought I was crazy.

"You're right. I will." I smiled at the thought of talking to my old friend again.

The next day we had earned a patio break and I made a beeline to the payphones. I called Nikki. The phone rang and rang with no answer. A small line had formed behind me at the pay phone, the other recruits wanting their turn. I had only made one call to my mother since arriving here. I was about to hang up when on the other end of the line I heard, "Hello?"

It was her.

"Hey, girl."

"Sasha, is that you? Girl, I have been thinking about you so much. I spoke to your mom the other day. She told me all the shit that went down. I can't believe you went off and joined the military. You are so freakin' extreme. Why haven't you called me?"

I took a deep breath, not sure how to tell her how I'd gotten here.

Luckily, she went on. "You could have just moved to New York with me. I'm doing all right. Guess my father had some abandonment issues, so he really hooked me up. I got a chill apartment, going to school, trying to break into video production and all that." She sounded pleased.

Her words stung a little. My parents never would have paid for an apartment for me. Instead, they asked me for money.

I considered hanging up and walking away. I didn't want to hear how great she was doing because it just made me feel bad about myself. But it was good to hear her voice. I did miss her, and I didn't want her to stop talking. Not knowing when or if I would talk to her again was enough to keep the phone plastered to my ear. I decided not to turn the conversation negative. I decided not to tell her I thought I was going mental.

"Hey, you still there?" she asked after a long pause.

"Oh yes, sorry. I'm... I'm happy for you." I tried to sound cheerful. "I'm in basic training now, should be done in about six more weeks. If I make it that long. I want to become a SERE specialist."

"A seer? That sounds like something my mother would want to do." She laughed.

"Ha, no, it's just S-E-R-E—Survival, Evasion, Resistance, and Escape specialist. Anyway, they won't tell me until the end of training if I'll get it, but I hope so."

"Sounds cool, I guess, if you like all that. I know I don't have it in me. But I know you do. You're tough, Sasha. You've always been tough. You'll make it. For sure." I pictured her, eyes intense with a warm smile, as she spoke. "Yo, so, how about those dreams—are you still having them?"

"Yeah, even more now." My voice quivered.

"Oh, no. That sucks. Ok, well you know you can always call my mom. She loves you and can help you figure that stuff out. You always had the strangest dreams."

Nikki's mother was a tarot card reader, healer and New Age spiritualist who'd taught me how to balance my chakras, center my energy and meditate. I went to her anytime I needed to understand some of the metaphysical craziness that'd appeared in my life.

"Mom always said our dreams are our greatest teachers. Something about the dreams themselves being our inner instincts and learning to navigate the world that surrounds us. Yeah. I remember now. She would say dreams allow us to weave together the seen with the unseen parts of us we hide, or just don't understand yet."

"Are you smoking a blunt?" I asked. She sounded trippy.

"Yeah, girl," she said in one soft, relaxed breath.

I heard agitated mumbling behind me and turned around. The misty Shadow was swirling lightly around the group, closer to some of the recruits than others.

"I've got to go, there's a line of people waiting to make calls." I kept my back to the crowd behind me. "But one thing has changed about my dreams lately." I gripped the receiver tighter now with both hands. Closing my body in, shoulders hunched over and head down, almost whispering, "I see those shadows when I'm awake, too."

"Oh, gurl, are you high now?" She laughed even louder. "What kind of drugs are they giving you in there? Ha. You got some military-issue crypto weed?" She let out another chuckle.

I laughed with her. At first it was a short, nervous laugh. Then I just let myself go and laughed like she was right there next to me.

"Right? Military-issue weed." I laughed again. "What I mean is, there are shady people in here, too, Nikki. It's like I've got a dark cloud following me wherever I go, and I can't shake it."

"Maybe you do, maybe you don't. Then again, maybe it's all just something you gotta go through. Life is like that, right? We need to experience certain things to get us where we're going. Look at all you've been through, and now look where you are. You left that asshole, you got fit and joined the military. Girl, you did a lot of things to get yourself where you are. Maybe you just had to go through all of that." The phone went silent for a few heartbeats. "We're all on our own paths. No two are the same."

I had never thought of it like that. I never once considered that I'd gotten myself here. Rather, it felt like I ended up here because I was running so fast, for so long.

Every choice I made was to escape a worse situation I saw unfolding before me. Not part of some master plan. Just survival. But she made it sound like I got some things right. At once my shoulders pulled back, and I stood with my head high.

"Ok, mama. Now I got to go. These people are getting restless. Thanks for the talk, my friend. Miss you."

"Miss you too, boo. Call me again when you can."

"I will." I hung up, smiling like I had not smiled in months. Damn, I missed her!

I turned around. A line of ten or so people stood behind me, the Shadow swirling around above them. I was not going to let this smoky, dark, depressing thing keep me down. Olvídate. I decided to walk directly through the mist with zero fear.

Surprisingly, the Shadow created an opening for me to walk through, parting in the middle and allowing me to pass. It didn't reach out to cloak me with dread like it had so many times before. This was new. And the only thing new about me was that I was happy—scratch that, proud—like I hadn't been in a long time.

Chapter 8

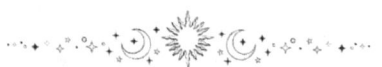

But that one positive moment was short-lived. Those damn Zodiac Shadows never stopped. They never took a day off. A cat-and-mouse game played in my mind, beginning as soon as I closed my eyes at night. In the minutes after lying down on the tight, military-issue dorm cot and before the blanket of sleep fell over me, I had to brace myself for what I knew would always come. But now I was even more determined to take back control of some aspect of my unstable mind.

Every day of training, we woke up at 4:00 a.m. and exercised. We carried hundred-pound packs for three miles around the base, ran obstacle courses, conducted weapons drills and learned things like the Law of Armed Conflict. This was such a far cry from the expectations I'd built up from reading all those books in high school and college. Magic academies where the main characters were tested based on some made-up abilities. Romances where the hot, alpha-hole bullies were secretly in love with the heroine.

I wish. This shit here was hard. Every part of my body was sore all the time, and there were zero magical healers waiting with some potion to ease all this pain. So, I had to focus on the pain. It was so pronounced it shot up through my muscles and throbbed there until nightfall. Then I did it all again the next day. But this pain helped me stop thinking so much about the darkness creeping into my soul.

Since I couldn't have my beloved books, I tried to remember places that made me happy as I drifted to sleep, like my Titi Lily's farm in Villalba. I brought each tiny detail to the forefront so that when I fell asleep, I could go to that place almost immediately. But I ran out of those memories; I had only so many. And sometimes the darkness would still find me.

Before my enlistment date, I'd watched a few travel shows and had tried to take in the details of the places that interested me. I committed the architecture, streets and landscapes to memory. I even imagined the smells there, all so I could escape the claws and demon eyes that reached for me every night.

As TI Grange turned the lights out in the dorm, I imagined myself standing at the edge of Castillo San Felipe del Morro, where the sea crashed like thunder against the centuries-old fortress walls. The ramparts stretched out into the Atlantic like a jagged crown, and the ancient sentry posts—the garitas—looked out over the dark water as if guarding secrets older than time. I pictured myself walking that stone path, where the breeze brought ancient whispers of battles, invasions and freedom fighters hell bent on claiming their independence. The echos of rebellion still lingered within its walls. A long sloping ramp curved up from the city below and I pictured myself walking this path as though it was calling me home. As I repeated these details over and over, sleep took hold.

I was flying over the ocean, and below me was the large expanse of El Morro's surrounding grass field. I felt compelled to fly even more forward, until I was beyond it's walls. My feet touched down lightly on the sandstone floor of Plaza de Armas where battles for freedom are never forgotten – etched into the canon-scarred walls. After a brief walk around the barren space, I settled against the edge of a ramp, soaking in the expanse of the Atlantic Ocean that stretched endlessly before me.

Time was not linear in this dream state, and at once I was in the past, present, and future. A menacing chill trickled down my spine as I noticed a movement in the distance. The dark clouds were rolling in.

It had found me.

My instinct was to run, fly away again, head to my goat shed in Villalba where I knew I was safe—but this time I didn't. It had been weeks since the Shadow had gripped me with unutterable fear. I had forgotten the dread the terrible darkness instilled in me. In the moment of its approach, I decided to stop running. I would confront the thing. I was not its mouse to be chased.

If I could reconstruct the goat shed in Villalba and the entire El Morro fortress, then I could reconstruct my weapon. Instantly I was holding the M-16 rifle from my training.

I was ready for whatever came next, and this time I wouldn't run.

The disturbingly familiar sound gripped me first, those high-pitched screeches in the distance. The low, inhuman howl rose in pitch as the darkness consumed everything, and I was surrounded by the charcoal mist, save only for the salt-stained rampart, bracing my back as the darkness closed in. I stood in a fighting position, ready for its worst.

At once, the deafening whispers ceased, and it was completely silent. I couldn't see anything except the rough stone wall behind me for what felt like an eternity. My impatience grew, and I ventured to take a look at the dark corridor to my right. There, emerging from the sloped ramp, appeared the hellish TI. He approached me at full attention, and I aimed my rifle as I was taught. He saluted me stiffly.

"What do you want?"

He looked at his saluting hand mockingly with his raw, primal eyes, then they locked with mine. He shrugged his shoulders and scoffed, like this was all some sort of joke.

"What in the world, Sasha?" The not-TI's voice had taken on a pretentious British accent, nothing like the Southern twang of his actual voice. He completed the sharp salute and relaxed his stance. "You thought you could escape our reach by joining the military? Surrounded by gates manned by security forces, tankers, ammunition, and fighter jets? It is, quite frankly, disappointing, and adorable at the same time, how naïve you still are. And I see you have a gun now. Just like Ares the War God to set this all up just so. Go ahead, knock yourself out."

He opened his arms wide and multiplied into one hundred versions of himself.

But something was different. As I looked closer at the faces, I saw familiar ones. Omar was to his right. Nikki to his left. My father. My brother. Even my mother. The judges, the police officers who'd arrested Omar. All of them were in the TI's military uniform with stern expressions. My senses were alert to every movement, and I prepared for a battle.

At once my older brother's torment stared me in the face.

I was back in my home in Miami, my mother casting me aside and praising him for yet another win. Another moment of glory.

In the next second, I was on my knees being arrested for shoplifting, then for marijuana possession.

Then I was opening a safe for the biggest mafia robbery I had ever done.

I was being slapped by Omar after showing up at the club one night after our wedding. He treated me as property, never as an equal.

Even the judge from my divorce was there, detached and unconcerned with my fate or anyone else's.

At the same time as I was being abused, I was also detached, an observer of the events. I saw the fear in my eyes, the depression that kept me from eating food that was right in front of me. The excitement of getting accepted into the military and finding a way out of my hellish life.

Now I realized it wasn't a way out. Instead, I was in over my head in its maddening bullshit.

As the multitude of TIs stood before me, I decided this was insufferable. I was not some weak, beaten woman they could torment as they pleased. Not now, and not ever again.

I took position, aimed and shot rounds into the chests of all the TIs in my line of sight. Unharmed, they only continued to multiply with more faces. Those prisoners and guards from Omar's prison, the recruits in my squadron, kids from my school.

Every single person who had impacted my journey was there, all of them threats ready to take me down. They multiplied until they crowded the entire Plaza de Armas inside the fortress.

My hands were slippery from the sweat and heat of discharging the weapon and the burn of the bullet casings as they flew out of the chamber. All my shooting did absolutely nothing.

"This ends here," I said, visibly shaking. "This ends with me. Right now. No more." I wished I hadn't just said that. I expected imminent death and wished it on myself if I couldn't kill them all.

"No, my dear, it is only the beginning. You've yet centuries to go," said whatever it was that had inhabited the likeness of Grange in this dream.

"This is bullshit. I want a normal life. What do you mean centuries? And are you telling me that you'll follow me, spewing your dark venom all over me for the rest of my life? Possessing the people around me so they turn against me?" I glared at all the faces. "I want to do the right thing. I am doing the right thing, now, finally. And here you are, turning me into a crazy person," I gasped in desperation, almost pleading now. "I'm seeing you while I'm awake... everywhere." I was breathing fast, panic rising in my voice.

"You only see what you want to see, Sasha. And it's charming." Grange's voice held the calm of Buddha. "Stubborn little soul, aren't you? Such a child. Still not able to see through the veil to who you really are. What you consider normal is an illusion. I expected you to have figured that much out by now." That face, no longer shrouded in darkness, looked pristine, angel-like, despite being annoyed. He had smooth, deep olive skin, contoured cheekbones and intense eyes that practically glowed a vibrant green. "You are the calm before the storm, the eye in its center, and the thing that will tear it all apart when it breaks."

"What in the stars are you talking about?" I gaped at him.

"I already told you these shadows are you. Control them, or they will destroy you. The dark will eat away at your mind like a parasite, and there won't be any of you left in there." The shadow form lifted a finger and tapped his temple two times. "Now get a grip."

He tilted his head as he considered me. "Given the extreme state of affairs, I've had to intervene," he continued. "Your shaman is still missing, and he is the only one who can help you cross the Gate."

"This shit with the shaman again. I don't even know who he is. How am I supposed to find him?" I asked.

He sauntered toward me as he spoke, knowing my weapon would do him no harm.

"Many will not want you to succeed, Estrellita. In fact, you should never have gotten this far. If it wasn't for all the work you've done on your own, you wouldn't have. They know who you are now, and they will keep coming after you."

"Who? Who is after me?" Sweat dripped from my brow.

"The factions that want to break through the Gates and feast on humanity. The nagual are the defenders of the Gates and are called the Gatekeepers. And these factions have been killing off nagual before they shift. I believe they have been trying to stop you from becoming a nagual since your birth. This is probably why your shaman has been missing. But we know he's alive. You must find him."

The not-TI looked around and I wondered who he really was. He knew my nickname. I was in such a state with all this information, I couldn't find the words to ask.

"You will be waking up soon," he said, his voice as loud as thunder. "The stars have spoken. Your Soul Contract must be fulfilled during the Transit of the Twelfth House, or you will be completely consumed by the darkness. Do not stop until you cross."

With his final words, the not-TI transformed into a serpent. I jumped back as the hundreds of remaining TIs changed shape to hundreds of serpents. At once, the serpents slithered down the sloping ramps and shadowy corridors before they disappeared, leaving me alone in the Plaza, looking out over a clear horizon.

Chapter 9

I opened my eyes in the safety of the cot, lying practically in the same position I'd fallen asleep in. My shirt was soaked with sweat, and I felt the urge to change it. This was a dilemma, because each shirt was accounted for. Here, we were allowed four T-shirts, but you only ever used two. We wore one and had one in the laundry, and the other two were always in the locker—ironed, folded and ready for inspection. I checked my watch, and the glow-in-the-dark face showed 3:15 a.m. Reveille would blast in a little under an hour.

The fifty women around me were completely silent. Not a snore or a grunt, yet the slightness of their inhales and exhales was comforting. I stared at the stark ceiling of dimmed fluorescent light panels and tried to make sense of my dream.

So much had just happened. I felt a richness in my chest, because this time I had not tried to escape the Zodiac Shadows. This was the first time since the dreams had taunted my waking life that I'd stood up to that fucker and tried to stop the torment. All this time, I fully expected it to take my life and integrate my soul with the hundreds or thousands I witnessed among its depths.

Conscious of even the slightest sound, I lifted off my shirt while still under the covers and stuffed it in the laundry bag hanging on the side of the bed. The mattress spring creaked, and I froze in place.

As I sat up, now shirtless, the cool air hit my skin and woke up my senses. When I saw not a single person stirred, I stepped out onto the cool concrete with the lightness of snowfall. I moved toward the locker, opened the door and slid out the notebook and pen. I visualized a feather as I retreated to the bed and exhaled in relief as there was not another creak from the bedsprings. I positioned myself so the notebook could capture the emergency light from the hallway.

I began to take notes.

What did I know about shadows? I had never heard of anyone seeing deadly shadows that haunted their dreams and their days. Unless they were psycho. Unless they were hallucinating. A fresh chill ran down my spine as I recalled all the sleepless nights tormented by the screeching shadow. The not-Grange had said that Shadow was me. **Me?** And who was I, after all? A nagual? A shapeshifter from the Underworld? What a ridiculous thought.

There were other forces at play here. My dreams had a deeper meaning. They were real. Everything that was happening was strangely real.

I had to start picking apart the Shadows I saw. The changes in the colors. Shifts of shapes. I would make it my secret project to learn more about the Zodiac Shadows, and in doing so, learn more about myself. After all, I was the darkness. And it was me. And I had a feeling there were others like me out there, somewhere.

I was stronger now. The military made me stronger. Facing the Shadow head-on made me stronger. I was beginning to believe in myself. To know that I didn't have to accept abusive men in my life. That no one would ever control me again. And that my future was entirely in my hands.

After staring death in the face and hearing its voice as persistently as I had over the past year, I knew there were only two places left for me to go. I could succumb to my greatest fears, or I could overcome them. Starting today, I would overcome them.

Seconds later, at exactly 4:45 a.m., reveille sounded. It was a new day.

Chapter 10

Four of us recruits were sitting silently, as usual, at our lunch table in the dining hall. We were not allowed to talk during mealtimes in basic training.

You only see what you want. Words from the dream last night had been repeating in my mind since I'd woken up that day. *You've got centuries to go. The shadows are you.* What did that mean?

The crazy thing was, I had a vision that Omar would be arrested before it happened. Now the shadows of my dreams were talking to me directly through people. Was that how this thing worked? The dark wall of doom showed me my future, then it happened? Was I receiving instructions about my life through my dreams? So, if that was true, then maybe TI Grange was my shaman! Maybe that had something to do with why I was so outrageously attracted to him. That could be why he'd shown up in my dream and spoken to me. I had to know.

The recruit next to me nudged my hand. "Snap out of it. Table one is about to get up, and Grange is watching you," she whispered, looking at her plate instead of directly at me.

I looked around the dining hall. This was the center of yelling and discipline for the TIs. They would search the crowd for the smallest slip-up. A recruit who chewed too long. A canteen hung from the side of the chair and not placed under it.

The hunger and exhaustion of the hundreds of recruits in that room made for a prime time of mistakes and excellent TI humiliation hunting. The height of the yelling was geared toward all the recruits in week zero. Now that we were in week two, we understood what was expected and fell in line more easily. I, however, was still reconciling the events of the previous night and was completely off my game.

We sat four to a table in the order that we left the cafeteria line, starting with table one. When the table before you got up, it meant you had to get up right after, because they were done eating and therefore you should be, too. And it was in this same order we would file out of the dining hall.

I was so lost in thought I hadn't eaten. I grabbed a hardboiled egg and shoved the entire thing in my mouth. Then I grabbed the roll and finished it in a single bite. The table next to me began to slide their trays and stand. I still had three electrolyte beverages on my tray I had to finish. It was required.

Brooding TI Grange eyed me with a hawk's dangerous precision, and I had to fight against every part of me that actually wanted him to hunt me. I could feel him searching for any opportunity to prove his power over me. From the darkness lurking around him, I could tell he was looking to find trouble. As he walked over to us, the girls at the table all responded to his arrival with freshly-arched backs.

I picked up the first drink and guzzled it down in less than five seconds. The recruits at table one, right next to our table, stood up. We were table two. I grabbed the second drink and finished it in another ten seconds. The recruits in table one shuffled out of their chairs and pushed them under the table. I grabbed the third drink and brought it to my lips. The recruits at my table disguised their anxious and excited looks with seriousness as the TI stood directly across from me, willing me to spill my drink.

I gulped the drink down as they waited, knowing these extra five seconds I took to devour the beverage were a demonstration of camaraderie and teamwork. I knew full well these women should have been standing the moment the recruits at table one had pushed in their chairs. I knew then that despite whatever power the TI had over our hormones, these girls had my back.

In a flash, I set down my glass and did something I never would have even the day before. I looked directly into the TI's eyes. He returned my gaze and doubled it up with a look that said he either wanted to destroy me, or devour me, then he made a sharp pivot to the right.

As I placed my tray and dirty plates with the others and walked out of the dining hall, Grange walked up behind me and told me to stop in my place.

"Turn around," he said in a relatively normal tone. Not the normal hellish yelling the TIs usually used when recruits did things they considered wrong.

I turned around to face him. He stared me up and down, and I fought against my aching desire for him. For a moment I wondered if he'd had the same dream I'd had the night before. Was he aware he'd come to me and given me all kinds of advice? His fiery eyes told me no. He had no clue.

"Beauty Queen, give me a slip right now." The words rolling off his tongue, ripe with sensuality.

"Yes, sir," was my reply but I wanted to say, "Yes, and can I show you how sorry I am in the dorms later?" But of course, I didn't.

I reached into my cargo pocket and retrieved one. These slips were little forms that were pulled by TIs for either positive or negative reasons. Once they were pulled, they were placed in the recruit's file. After hearing from some of the recruits further along in their training, I was sure they weren't a big deal, but you didn't want them getting pulled for negative things too much. Too many pulled slips could result in getting kicked out.

Grange stood in front of me with his god-like perfect features, waiting. Heat pulsed through me as I recalled the taste of him on my tongue. My mind filled with a vision of me pulling off his shirt and making my way quickly down his ripped stomach. I bit my lower lip and looked hungrily into his eyes.

"This is for goat roping while everyone else was eating their lunch." His tone was the exact opposite of reprimanding. In fact, it sounded like he was just using this whole moment as an excuse to talk to me longer.

If this was the outside world, I would write my number on this little paper and tell him to call me later.

When I handed him the slip, my finger felt an electric pulse as it grazed his. I breathed in a broken breath. I remembered the plan, which was to find my shaman. When I was little, my Titi Lily had given me a tarot card and had said it was my birth card. It was "The Magician." She said The Magician was real, and he was my shaman. It occurred to me to ask Grange if he was The Magician, since it would sound a little less crazy than asking if he was my shaman.

"Sir, are you The Magician?"

He flinched, but his eyes gave nothing away. "I'm not a magician, but I can make this little slip disappear if you behave yourself. You're dismissed." Thank fuck. Grange isn't my shaman. That would have been so awkward!

I left the dining hall and walked right out into a bright, beautiful, sunny day. To my pleasant surprise, my tablemates were waiting for me. We walked together to formation. I saw a shimmering glow on everyone around us, and it was beautiful.

"You were lost in space, you know." Speed laughed and lightly bumped my shoulder with her fist.

I'd never noticed her bright smile before. She was one of those tall, long-legged farmer girls I thought I had nothing in common with. Today I saw her differently, more clearly and surrounded by a deep magenta glow that seemed familiar.

"How did you drink those down so fast?" asked Cook, glittering in both yellow and orange. Something about these colors I was seeing reminded me of my childhood.

"Oh, well, lots of practice chugging in drinking games back home." A comfortable smile warmed my face.

We joined up with the rest of the recruits and waited before taking our places in formation. After the others finished lining out of the dining hall, we would all march to our classrooms. Military History was first, then Combat Command Organization.

"You guys didn't have to do that back there," I said. "He could've pulled all your slips along with mine." Even though I felt this compulsive attraction to TI Grange, I was still very aware there were strict rules we all had to follow, and I didn't want anyone to get in trouble because of me. "But... Thank you."

Since I began boot camp, the recruits around me buzzed along like bees in a hive. I saw them. I heard them. But they faded into the background. They were blurry and could sting me if I provoked them; they could even turn against me. They were seen and unseen at the same time.

But something changed that day, and I realized these recruits were humans. They weren't enemies, my competition, or threats. Just now at breakfast, they were there for me. I didn't even care I had a slip pulled. For the first time, I wasn't alone in this place.

"If he pulled my slip, it would've been worth it. Grange is a complete douche." Santos spoke up for the first time ever. She was radiating an opalescent blue. Her thick New York accent reminded me of some friends back home, the ones that had moved down to Miami.

I turned to get a good look, studying her energy in more detail. Slim with an athletic build, Santos had very straight black hair pulled back into a bun and enviable, dark caramel skin. She was the one who'd bumped me with her shoulder after I'd made them wait in their sweat-drenched clothing in the stairwell.

"Yeah, he is the devil," I said. "No joke. That's the problem with the devil—he hides in plain sight."

Even though I was in some bizarre trance for Grange, I knew he was scandalous. There was that shit he pulled with the knife and how the dark mist lingers and grips on to him. He was just as shady as I was, and I had to admit it.

"He gives me the creeps." Santos lifted and shook her shoulders as if a chill had just run down her spine.

"I wish he would look at me like that." Cook giggled as she swooned over him. "That man is a tall drink of iced tea."

Santos looked away, and I rolled my eyes.

I recognized that gesture. Santos looked like I used to feel. Avoiding. Running. And as she spoke about him, her color shifted from a brightly lit blue to a shade of lifeless blue-gray. As I watched the hues shift right in front of me, I was sure then of what I had suspected earlier in the day: I wasn't just seeing the Shadow anymore. I had started seeing changes of color in people.

Colors blended and shifted around each person. I studied them. While there were just a few cadets and TIs around us who were almost entirely consumed by the Shadow, there were others where it only just circled over them. What did that mean?

Chapter 11

There was only one explanation for all this. I must be living in an alternate reality from everyone else. And in this alternate reality—that I was apparently alone in—I had to survive. I had to find a way to make this all tolerable as well as make a life for myself.

I pushed down feelings of self-pity. There was no time to ask, "Why is this happening to me?" or "Why can't I be like any other normal human who doesn't see soul-wrenching Shadows taking over the earth?" There was only time to figure out what to do now that I was here and take one more step forward.

As we stood in a small group in one corner of the outdoor pavilion, I made a mental note that the dark mist didn't hang out anywhere near these three women. They were bright. They were almost glowing as we stood together.

I checked in with myself and how I was feeling. Despite being harassed again by our TI, I realized it felt good speaking to these girls. In fact, after they'd waited for me to finish my drinks in the dining hall—as I subconsciously, or consciously, challenged the TI—I felt I could trust them. Remembering the way Santos's light had dampened, I made the decision to confide in her.

I stood close to Santos and approached her when the others were out of earshot. "Santos, watch out for the TI," I said. "He cornered me the other day. Lied."

Her eyes widened. She barely knew me. Why would she believe me? In that instant, I regretted saying anything. "Threatened you? How?" she asked.

"It's crazy. Yesterday, when I ate breakfast before everyone, he got me alone in the dorms. He said I had a knife in my luggage, and I knew he was using it to threaten me."

"He cornered me, too."

I knew there'd been something going on with her. "How? When?"

"Line up!" yelled Grange.

As the day went on, we had no time to continue our conversation. There was too much to do between preparing for our first inspection to finishing our classes and keeping up with our job details. But I had a lot of time to watch. I watched the Shadow and studied its movements. I saw the twisted, tortured souls inside its depths. I wouldn't run from them. I would learn from them. Their centuries of torture, pain and eternal suffering had lessons for me.

I loved how now I could also see all the lights. The colors gleaming from several of the recruits made me feel lighter. A memory surfaced, and I remembered Nikki's mom telling me these were auras, the colors of the energy that shot out from our seven chakras.

Jokes were rare around here, but whenever there were good ones, sparks flew around the people enjoying them. I had to wonder why I'd begun seeing the lights again after so long. Had they been here all along? Was I so consumed with my hysteria that I had missed them? Or did I unlock some sort of ability to see them by confronting the dark? Either way, the contrast between light and dark was even starker now. I was glad to know there even was a light, because all I saw before was darkness.

That night as I was making my way back to my bed, I saw Santos leaving Grange's office in the back of the dorm. Her head was down and shoulders slouched. The colors surrounding her were pale gray and black, but I knew the Shadow didn't have her because there was no depth to the colors—they were flat.

I walked toward the center aisle to check in with her and let her know I wanted to finish our conversation about him. She almost walked right past me, so I reached out my hand to get her attention, and she snapped her arm back before I could touch her. Her eyes lifted to meet mine, and she looked like a caged bird pleading to be free.

Her intensity eased just a bit, and she said, "He won't stop."

She shot a glance behind her, then turned and walked away. As she passed, I glanced at her neck. Her hair was pulled back into a braid so it was exposed. The tiniest drop of blood was on her collar, and two dark indentations faded into her natural skin right before my eyes.

I moved right through weeks three and four without any incidents with Grange, but I couldn't say the same about week five.

I kept my head down and focused on learning what they taught me while I studied the Shadow and the Light. There were times when the wind blew a certain way and even the trees would glisten with a golden glow. The Light was not just on people. It was everywhere.

The dark mist coexisted with the tree above it as the tree waved carelessly in the breeze, giving off electric golden hues.

The Light promised balance to the bleak view of the world around me. A cadet would laugh, a TI would be teaching a subject with passion, or a recruit would reach out their hand to help me up over an obstacle in one of our drills, and the Shadow would get quiet as the Light would shine. I studied what I saw in the tiniest of details, counting the tiniest of changes within the colors, noting any shifts.

Grange's tendrils of darkness creeped in and around him, a constant companion. I saw it more clearly the more I studied him. No one else I came across looked even as remotely devoured by the darkness as he was. Sure, some of the people here, male and female alike, had lower-light hues than others, and even more had darker hues, but their shadows were nothing compared to his.

One of the male recruits stood out from the others. His light would shift drastically from one color to another in short intervals. I timed it once, and his color shifted from purple to red three times within ten minutes. Everyone else I watched had consistency in their color most of the day, only getting brighter or duller depending on what we were doing or where we were. But his reminded me of a slow warning light, flashing on and off.

He was quiet and reserved and wouldn't interact much with the people around him. During our drills, I made excuses to get close to him to see if I could make sense of what I was seeing. Then at lunch, after we were each handed a prepackaged meal (or, in military-speak, MREs—Meals, Ready to Eat.), our options were either to stand in the blistering hot sun and eat or sit on the blistering hot pavement and eat. He decided to sit, so I joined him. His name tag read Baine.

When I sat next to him, I felt a certain electric energy, like a static charge, coming from him the closer I got. He had the look of someone who loved the outdoors. Strong jawline, sun-kissed bronze skin, sandy blond hair, blue eyes, tall and muscular. I pegged him for a surfer type from California. I had to admit, he was definitely hot. I hoped he wouldn't be one of those cocky types that were so hot on their own looks they expected girls to pine over them. At that moment, all I wanted was to understand what I was seeing.

Chapter 12

"Oh great, it's mystery meat again," I said, opening my aluminum bag of food. "My favorite."

He laughed. "Oh yeah, my favorite, too."

I wanted to ask him what he was thinking about, like I asked Cook, but I figured that'd just be weird. His colors kept changing. Purple to red. Red to purple. We ate in silence, pouring the food into our mouths with no fork or spoon, as we usually did on field days.

"Looking forward to that Snickers bar for dessert?" I asked.

"No, I don't really like Snickers. You can have mine if you want."

I decided he definitely had a California accent.

"Oh no, that's ok. One Snickers is enough. I've got to watch my figure; these uniforms are revealing," I joked, tugging at the camouflage fabric of my shirt.

They were the opposite of revealing.

He chuckled, but his colors never changed. Still just purple, then red. I thought if he laughed, the colors would lighten or shift in hue or balance out. But I was wrong.

"So, we made it to week five. Only two more weeks to go." I was fishing for some more insight.

"Yeah, it's almost over. I wonder where we'll all get stationed." He looked directly at me, eyebrows raised.

I saw something in his eyes. I couldn't yet place it, but yes, there was something else there. There was a sadness, a darkness there, like I had seen many times in the green eyes staring back at me from my mirror.

"No idea, but I'm ready to get the hell out of here," I said.

"You see it, too."

My heart jumped, and my pulse quickened. Could he know about the Shadow? "See what?"

"See the end to daily boot camp torture and the days of mystery meat."

"Oh, yeah." I let out a nervous laugh. "Yeah, of course."

"What career detail are you going for?"

"I'm hoping to become a SERE."

"Me, too. That's exactly what I requested. You're the only other person I've talked to here who even knows about that detail."

"Interesting." I wondered if that mere coincidence was what I had picked up on. "Good luck."

"Same to you."

Just then, the TI announced we had five minutes to finish lunch and use the latrines. There was still much for me to learn about his colors. I would have to talk to him later to figure it all out. My day went on like that, studying people, asking simple questions to test my theories, taking notes, and growing in confidence.

CHAPTER 13

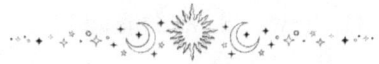

The line formed behind me, and, to my relief, they were all laughing and relaxed. No dark Shadow looming above or in the corners. I had time.

I was on a patio break and had just finished talking to my mother. I had spoken to her every other week since I joined. When we spoke, our phone calls were short, and she asked the same questions each time. How was I doing? Was I eating? Would I graduate? Each time I answered, "Yes," and gave her all the details about the graduation.

She said she would try to come, but I knew she couldn't afford the flight and hotel. In all the time I'd been here, I'd never thought she was proud of me. As I hung up the phone and turned around, I must have been smiling, because the recruit who passed me flashed a cheesy smile of his own.

We still had twenty minutes left on our break, so I grabbed a snack and a soda from the vending machines and sat down on one of the benches next to Santos. I looked up into the twilight sky, wondering what my mother was doing with herself now that my brother and I were out of the house. As I gazed upon the purple-and-pink evening canvas, I hoped Dante wasn't drinking too much and paying some attention to her, but I doubted it. I took a bite of my Snickers.

"Where are you from?" Santos asked, snapping me out of my daydream.

"Miami," I said.

"I'm from the Bronx."

As she sat there, asking me questions, the tips of the gray outline of her Light—I mean aura—took on a looming shade of doom that slithered like snakes into the beautiful cobalt blue that made up most of the glow surrounding her. There it was—the Shadow creeping into an otherwise nonthreatening person. It made me uneasy, and I had the urge to run, but I knew I didn't have to. The Shadow was not after me. But still, there was something menacing about it.

"Listen, I know you probably don't want to talk about this," I began. "But what happened with you and the TI? You can tell me."

After her reaction to me in the dorms, I expected she knew this conversation was coming. I wondered if she would avoid me and pull away like she had in the dorm that day. So, I worked on shifting my energy to white, because I knew white energy would be the most comforting.

She looked up into the sky and then down at the chips in her hands. "I've only ever been with one guy, my boyfriend from back home since tenth grade. We messed around, but we never 'did it.' We were waiting to get married. He joined the service, too. He started basic before me and graduates this week. We plan to get married after we both graduate. But now, nothing feels right." She shook her head, then moved her hand to cover her stomach. "What happened with the TI makes my stomach sick. Now I feel guilty every time I talk to Benny." Her forehead was furrowed, and her lips were pursed tight.

My brows pinched at the center. "But what exactly happened with him?"

Her face turned to stone, and she looked away. "Something I don't want to talk about."

"Look, I get it. The TI is like... irresistible on every level. And I've had fantasies in just about every position, on every surface with him. Seriously, no judgement."

I kept a hold of the white energy I used to cover us. I resisted the impulse for it to shift gray and black with the thoughts of what had happened.

She seemed to soften. "I love Benny, more than anything. But for some reason I was so attracted to Grange the second I saw him, I forgot all about my boyfriend. All I could think about was him. He was the most beautiful man I had ever seen, and my body, it just like... It rages for him. Bad." Her eyes bulged as if this whole idea shocked her. "So, one day, when he was in his office, he excused everyone but me, and I swear, it was like something else controlled me." Her voice started shaking. "I don't know what came over me! Ever since then I've felt so guilty for betraying my boyfriend. I love him! I didn't mean to do this to him or to us."

She looked into my eyes, insisting I understand.

"Why don't you say anything?" I asked quietly. "Report him?"

"Why don't *you* report him?" she snapped back, shaking her head. "One minute I was alone with him in his office, and the next *I* was all over *him*. The second it was over I realized how much this would hurt Benny. When I came to my senses and pulled away, he told me the same thing he told you. But instead of a knife, he threatened me with cocaine. You think I want to get thrown out of here? I need this."

"I need this, too. I don't have anywhere to go if this doesn't work. This is my last chance to get my life together," I said.

Santos shook her head. "I guess we're both fucked."

"How does he get away with this?" I wondered out loud. "There must be thousands of recruits passing through here. If this is going on with us, he must have done this before, to others."

"Because who wouldn't want him?" She sat straighter now, her eyes narrowed. "The second I get close to him, it's like I can't stop myself." She rubbed her neck.

"Why are you rubbing your neck like that?"

"Oh, it's just sore. It's been bothering me since, well, you know."

"Can I look at it?"

She moved closer to me and turned her head to the side. I inspected the area and found it a little bruised under the surface, but that was all. I remembered the way he put pressure on my neck that day when I was alone with him. The pain of a pierce, then a pull through my skin. I'd quite enjoyed it, and a warmth rose within me at the memory.

"I wonder what it is about him that makes him so hard to resist." The part of me that fought to restrain myself from my own desires for him wanted to know. That small, quiet voice deep inside me that knew he wasn't at all like other men.

"I have no idea."

Black energy creeped further into her colors, and I felt the same happening to me. All I could do was shake my head.

Chapter 14

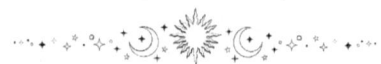

I closed my eyes that night with images of Villalba vivid in my mind. I needed to regroup. The once small and rotting goat shed I would escape to was now bigger and built of the same cedar wood as the benches and walls of the patios at the base. My mental refuge was now furnished with large, colorful floor pillows and a comfortable, soft blanket. Long white curtains hung from the ceiling and brushed the floor beside the two large openings overlooking the mountains and lake.

Now that I looked around, it seemed like I had recreated a spa I'd once seen on one of the travel channels, complete with two macrame basket lights hanging from the ceiling. I settled in one of the blankets and closed my eyes to meditate.

I had to take a minute to work out what to do about the TI. I couldn't stand the idea of him doing this to us again, doing this to other women and getting away with it. I murmured the mantra *So Hum*. I had read some meditation books that Nikki's mom gave me and they had taught me all about mantras. This one was simple and easy to remember, so I used it a lot. It just meant, "I am."

In my pleasant headspace, I focused on what Nikki's mom had taught me about opening my chakras to make sure none of the discs were blocked. Aligning and unblocking these energy discs would open the wisdom of each energy point, and in my case, I was sure it was opening up my visions. After I was realigned, I concentrated on the TI.

Still sitting in a meditative position in my comfortable cabana in Villalba, I recalled how his Shadow moved. It clung to him and expanded out from his center. Unlike the auras I saw, which surrounded the individuals, his was more of a projection outward. I tried to follow the advice of all those creepy life coaches and sent him wishes for peace and calm. I imagined him surrounded by a white aura, but as the white energy tried to penetrate his, it bounced back, slammed me in my chest, and left my breath caught in my throat. I choked on the white energy and coughed it up. Geez, so much for sending love to whatever he was.

I tried with the other colors, and one by one they were all rejected except for gray. There was no bouncing back, no clear rejection. But there was no acceptance either. Then I tried black. That energy blended right into his and there I was, in his inner world.

His inner world smelled of a deep, rich musk. The corners and edges were pitch black, and the center glowed with a crimson light. I thought I heard subdued screams, moans of ecstasy and then a deep rip somewhere off in the distance. That was when I saw him, bare-chested and rippling with muscle. His torso, arms and chest seemed carved from stone, and his face was dark and tempting. My insides betrayed me at the sight of him, and my core throbbed with desire.

He was in a large room; it looked like it could be his apartment. The furniture was modern, and the sheets a shiny black satin. He had a woman in the bed I didn't recognize, and she wore black, lacy lingerie. Her hair was thick, light brown and curly, and she worked her way up his ripped abs. Another woman was behind him, massaging his glutes and wrapping her perfectly manicured hands across his chest. The black-laced woman kissed him hungrily, but he pulled away. He tilted her head to the left and moved her hair to expose her neck.

His mouth revealed two sharp fangs that snapped out and sank deep into her skin. He pulled and pulled from her neck, and blood streamed down her shoulder and the line of her back to her waist. Then as though I was seeing a different memory in another corner of his mind, I saw him in the dorms with a woman wearing a military uniform and sitting on top of his desk. He stood there between her legs, rocking back and forth with blood-stained lips as though he had already taken in his fill of her blood.

There were flashbacks of him carrying out his impulses when he was younger, perpetual reenactments floating like clouds in his mind. His high school and college days were plagued by rotting corpses. He wore a football jersey and stood over a bloodied woman's body that lay distorted on the floor.

I flinched, trying to make sense of what I saw. My brain told me I should be disgusted, but instead, all I wanted was to see more.

I tried not to create too much of a stir, as I didn't want him to notice an intruder in whatever place this was. But honestly, it seemed he would never suspect it. The energy was as toxic as it was alluring. I was drawn to his obsession. I couldn't stop myself from watching, his impulses overpowering me. The excitement he felt as he looked in the young women's desperate eyes was now my excitement. The control and power he felt in getting away with carrying out his primal desires was now my power and my control. Control I had never had and very much wanted. Rather than become an intruder, I became an accomplice to these deviant acts he relished.

Still curious, I kept watching, not sure what I was looking for. I saw him as a child, maybe four, dirty in a filthy home, crying on the floor while a woman lay sleeping on the bed above him, immune to his cries. He fussed on the floor with a toy and threw it against the wall. She stirred in her bed and when she did, he grabbed her arm. She swatted him away, but he yanked at her even harder.

He soiled himself, a brown liquid oozing down his leg. He cried louder. She sat up and took his hand.

Walking him into her dark, cluttered closet, she closed the door behind him. "Time for a nap, Mikey." The woman returned to bed and sat on its edge. From the drawer of her nightstand, she removed a syringe and meticulously filled it with a liquid from a tiny white bottle. She injected it in between her toes and laid back in bed as Mikey's cries turned to a soft whimper behind the closet doors.

Then I saw him walking out of a gas station with some groceries in a plastic bag. It was dark, and he stood staring off at the long, empty road that was his walk home.

The high-pitched whisper buzzed in my ear again, and I knew a presence was nearby.

A young woman about his age appeared at the edge of the gas station, huddling in a shadowy corner. Her clothing was stained with blood, and her eyes held a blank stare.

"Hey, Melanie," he said, coming over to her. "What's wrong?"

When he got close, she held his face in her hands and locked her gaze with his. She opened her mouth and revealed two lines of sharp, yellow-and-black teeth that could have never belonged to any human.

"I won't make it like this," she whispered.

She looked at long scratches on her arms. That familiar dark mist formed into tornados all around her and channeled into her body, then through her eyes into his. She took a deep bite into his neck and pulled in his blood. Finished, her knees buckled under her, and she fell to the ground.

He quickly placed his hand on his neck. When he pulled his hand away, it was sticky with red blood that seeped from his neck. He stared at his blood for many heartbeats, then looked at her lifeless body on the ground.

He walked home in a daze and saw a middle-aged, heavy-set man in a flannel shirt walk out his front door and open his car door. On impulse, Mikey ran toward him with a supernatural speed and pulled him into the shadows of the house. The man struggled but couldn't break free of his grip, and Mikey bit into his flesh.

I heard the man's bones breaking. My mouth watered as the taste of blood became a deep craving inside my very own mouth.

I repeated the mantra So Hum, and detached myself from the horror of the scene I had just witnessed. I had never seen anything so wild in my life. I began to question my sanity, but I pushed the thoughts away. I had to accept that what I saw could be true. That Michael Grange wasn't of the human world.

And then I caught a glimpse of myself, another me, across a dark room. It was week zero, and I was about to do what he was asking me to do right before his fellow TIs showed up and stopped us. But this time I did what he wanted, and he didn't care about the interruption.

The energy around this image was different from the others. It was fuzzy, blurry and dull. I could only imagine the fuzziness meant that this was something he still desired. Then I saw Santos there with us, wearing her blue uniform. We were only supposed to wear our blues during the graduation week of training.

She sat in the room with Grange and me as I did exactly what he wanted me to do. He pointed for her to kneel next to me. The energy surrounding me—the observer-me in the back of the room—shifted from black to red, and bolts of energy like lightning shot out from my center. From a distance, the observer-me yelled, "No!"

Everything stopped.

Chapter 15

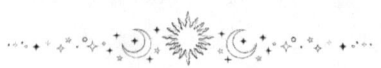

I heard a sharp, loud ringing in my ears. I lifted my hands to muffle the painful noise and noticed they were bright red. I repeated the mantra again, *So Hum*, and brought myself back to match the black energy of the room. The TI looked up just as I had completely faded back into the background. He grimaced, but he seemed more bothered about being interrupted than suspicious. After all, who infiltrates dreams?

He went back to what he was doing, the scene blurry, not as crisp as the others had been. He had Santos on his desk, her neck exposed, and he was about to bite. That's when I knew he wasn't done with us. He would try to do this again, to both of us.

I stepped backward as I watched, careful not to place my foot down too heavily and intent on remaining connected to the same low-energy frequency that belonged to Grange. I kept my pace steady, and I focused on the things I had in common with the monster: my desires for dominance and control and the idea of getting away with something impulsive in this stringent military environment. Like bashing his head in.

It was clear to me now that this was where he and I were not so different. By focusing on what we had in common, I could penetrate his thoughts and dreams without disturbing them. But if I changed my frequency, rejected his desires or tried to stop them, I would become an intruder and be exposed.

As I returned to the tranquil goat-shed-turned-spa-retreat, I slowly opened my eyes. So, I'd swapped a life dominated by a drug dealer for one now controlled by a man in uniform—possessed by a supernatural being, no less. A supernatural being that could lure women with a glance.

Even as it dawned on me that he had been turned by that cursed vampire kid Melanie, I had to fight a wild voice in my head that told me it didn't matter what he was. My body ached for his touch and demanded he satisfy all my desires.

My mind flashed to an image of that woman who'd been on his desk, only now it was me. I was running my palms up the deep contours of his bare chest and feeling the heat of his body pulsing against mine. I reached for his hand, the one that was holding the small of my back and moved it up my shirt to caress my breast. His fiery eyes looked deep into my soul, and all I wanted was the pleasure his touch could bring me. I shifted my gaze to the fangs hiding just beneath his lips and felt my mouth water with the urge to have them sink into the thick of my flesh. I pulled him closer now, my free hand reaching down to feel the length of his sex beneath his pants. I slid my hand down to feel him skin to skin.

No, I heard the faintest part of me say inside this fantasy. *Yes*, I returned in a heated breath, no longer in my goat shed but lying in my cot with my hand sliding down my stomach to feel the warmth growing between my thighs. *This is a trap*, I heard myself say a little louder. As though waking from a dream, I looked around. Forty women surrounded me, fast asleep in their cots.

How did he do this? There must be spells, voodoo, or santeria he performed on Santos and I, to make us want him so badly. And from what I'd seen from vampire movies, he probably did it so he could feed off our blood and enjoy it. A fire rose in my chest while my inner folds held on to the lingering desire. I focused on the burn of the fire that ignited deep in my root chakra, and it slowly replaced my lustful desires with fury. I had to tell everyone who and what he was!

Lashing out at him, turning him in or rebelling against him during the day were all tempting options. But on second thought, no one would believe me—I had no proof. It was his word—a fifteen-year sergeant's—against a newbie with a tarnished track record. Anything I did to him would lead to me being sent home, and there was no way that was happening.

I took a deep breath and returned to the goat shed in my mind. I got up and went for a swim in the lake behind the goat shed, working to clear my head and cool the flames growing within. While I was wading in the crystal-clear oasis between the mountains, I felt a little calmer, but I was still unsettled as I thought about the TI. I stepped out of the water, completely naked and fully in control of this scenic realm inside of me.

It was never too hot nor too cold here. There would be no trespassers because it was designed with a sense of nothingness. No attachments, no expectations of any specific outcome and no need to shut anyone out or let anyone in. It was in this state of allowing and lack of resistance that I was truly protected from the intrusion of fear, insecurity and uncertainty. I was at peace.

Remembering the rules that governed this serene harbor of mine, I simply allowed myself to be my true self and shifted into a black jaguar. That was when I realized I, too, was a beast of a different kind. They told me I was a nagual—a shapeshifter meant to be taught by a shaman. Now I believed them, and maybe it wouldn't be true in the real world, but here in my mind, I could be anything I wanted.

I padded around the deep blue lake, at home in my jaguar skin and at one with my surroundings. I crouched down on a large rock that jetted out into the lake as the nagual and peered into the water at my reflection. There was something different about my aura now—it was completely red. Usually it was red with an outline of purple. After I'd watched for about a minute, it flashed completely purple. Just like the sun-kissed recruit I'd spoken to earlier in the day.

There must be a reason for this, I considered as I lifted my gaze from the water to the horizon. At this moment I was projecting the same energy he was. My thoughts turned to him, to Baine. Concentrating on him and attaching any emotion to what I was experiencing would block rather than open the alignment of our connection. Again, I would allow the connection to present itself to me rather than be the one to chase it down.

With the grace of the jaguar, I returned to the goat shed. The path from the lake was wide and covered with a soft, black mulch that cushioned my steps along the way. It was lined with decorative rocks, orchids and other tropical flowers. One could hear the soft music of the coqui among the surrounding foliage at dusk while the sky was painted with purple, pink and yellow.

As soon as I entered the shed, I was back in my human form, my body cloaked in a long, white embroidered dress that fell to my knees with a drawstring waist and a flounced hem. I returned to my meditative position on the large mandala cushion in the center of the shed and closed my eyes.

So Hum, I repeated as I envisioned my reflection in the lake. My mind worked best with facts.

If I concentrated on one detail I knew to be absolutely true and not just what I wanted to believe to be true, more facts would reveal themselves. This truth had to abide by certain universal rules just like this peaceful harbor. To know something to be true, I had to have witnessed it with my own eyes. Any related details couldn't be guesses or suspicions, only concrete facts. In my desperate attempts to distinguish the world I knew from the world of Shadows, this was the only way I could make sense of anything. This was how I got through my darkest days when I'd begun seeing the Shadow.

Chapter 16

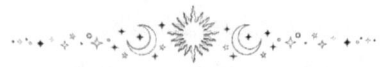

I recalled the memory of my aura flashing from red to purple, my face in its center. Then it flashed back, purple to red, and as it did, Baine's face replaced mine. It was like looking at him from one side of the mirror as he looked at himself while shaving in his dorm latrine. He wiped down his face with a white towel, turned off the faucet, then walked away from the mirror. As he did, his image faded, so I moved my energy through the mirror, attaching my red energy to the red around him, just as I had attached the black energy to the black around the TI.

If it worked for the TI, it should work for Baine—and it did. I became a part of his process and saw everyone was settling down for bed in the male dormitory. I could observe him from a distance as I joined with the other red energy of the room. The colors I saw around people also lingered as currents in the surrounding environment, streaming between the other bright colors of matched auras and avoiding the dark shadows.

What I saw depended on where I focused my energy. I had the urge to bounce into other energy streams to see what they felt like, but I had to focus on Baine.

I felt the environment around him as part of his own energy field within the red spectrum. I watched the blurry, fuzzy image unfold as he pulled back the bedding on his cot. He was about to climb in when the dorm guard approached and said something. I only heard muffled words, but I could tell from the look on Baine's face that whatever was said wasn't good.

Baine's face darkened, and he shook his head, shoulders hunched and his hand clenched into a fist. With his head down, he went to his locker to grab his boots. He slid them on and laced them up. Then he followed the dorm guard into the TI's office. His TI sat there with his brows softened, a slight tilt to his head and a look I wasn't used to on these stone-faced warriors.

The TI motioned for Baine to sit down, and as the TI spoke, the voices were still muffled. The TI's colors were green and blue. I focused on these colors and shifted mine to match, and it worked! I could hear him clearly.

"They think she won't make it through the night, and they want you to come home. We booked a flight for you to leave tomorrow at 0640, courtesy of the Red Cross." Baine's TI sat forward in his chair, leaning his elbows on the table.

"Look, you're one of my top cadets. You've aced academics, physical training, and have shown us all that you're a disciplined, stellar recruit. If you can make it back by this Friday, I've already cleared it with the base commander that you can reintegrate into this flight and graduate with the rest of the squad next week. This isn't how we normally handle these kinds of emergencies. We normally recycle the recruit and make them start with the next available flight. But because of your performance, we can make an exception. If you need more time while you're there, that's ok, but you won't graduate with this company."

I crept away from the TI and went back to matching the red energy surrounding Baine. I wanted to understand what was going on in his mind.

I saw flashes in his memory, scenes of a loving embrace with a woman with beautiful, long blond hair. She was wearing a green maxi dress in a perfectly manicured, lush green backyard with modern patio furniture. There was a pot roast at the center of the table with other family members filling the chairs.

A streamer nearby read, *Good Luck*. It seemed like a going away party for Baine. I turned my attention to another memory, where the woman and Baine sat in the patio chairs playing a card game. She could've been in her early or mid-fifties, maybe his mother. Then the same woman lay in a hospital bed, alone with tubes in her mouth and her beautiful blonde hair plastered against the pillow.

Baine nodded. "I'll do what I can to be back by Friday."

"Good plan, son. Wear your dress blues," replied the TI.

"Yes, sir."

Part of me wanted to stay and keep listening, but this had gotten too personal too fast, and it was time for me to go. I disengaged my energy slowly so I wouldn't disrupt the energy field around me.

It was easier to retreat from Baine than it'd been from Grange, maybe because I wasn't trying to match his red energy, as that came naturally for me. I didn't have to look for things in common; they were already there. We had the same passion for making it out of basic, the same drive to do something greater, the same feeling of accomplishment for getting as far as we both had, and all of this resounded in the red energy we exchanged freely.

Still in the safety of my lucid dream, I opened my eyes where I was sitting on the huge cushion in the goat shed. I began to contemplate what I saw and why.

One thing that stood out to me about the vision with Baine was that the TI had said Baine could still graduate with the rest of the squad next week. His fleet was our brother fleet, and we were set to graduate together, not next week but three weeks from now. Did that mean I'd just seen the future? As I tried to make sense of all this, I remembered the visions of Santos and me when I'd entered the TI's energy. Were those just erotic fantasies or the future?

This vision just now with Baine was not as straightforward. I didn't know him, and this personal situation of his had nothing to do with me. I was even more confused than when I'd started, and I was getting nowhere. I closed my eyes and allowed my mind to drift into deep sleep until reveille.

Chapter 17

Another day, another drill under the Texan sun, and we were just two weeks away from completing basic training. The days grew shorter and cooler as winter creeped in. We had just finished the one-and-a-half-mile obstacle course that now took us half the time to finish compared to the first time around. We were all physically improved, using parkour techniques to balance on the ropes, climb inverted walls and slide right through the military crawl.

While hanging upside-down on the double pullover bars, I saw Baine on the rope climb, the obstacle right after mine. There he was, hanging from the first knot at the very top of the rope, about to touch the wood frame. I had to catch up with him. The dark mist still crept in the corners, in the crevices and the shadows. I pulled it toward me, as if on instinct, like the demon vampire creature had done in my vision of TI Grange. Instead of running, instead of hiding from the fear I had of that darkness, I called it to me. It's power surged through me, as though it was coming home.

I had already reached the higher bar and placed my knees on the lower bar. I reached over the top bar to grab the lower bar with my palms outward and spun around the bar to dismount it.

I bolted to the rope climb and reached the top in record speed, touched the wood frame and tried not to slide down the rope too fast to avoid friction burns on my hands. At the bottom, I searched for him on the next obstacle, the log wall. His elbows were already propped on the top of the wall, ready to pull himself up.

I raced and jumped like a grasshopper, reaching the top with both hands in one easy sprint.

He glanced back at me from the corner of his eye as he made his way over. I took the same approach with my elbows and lifted my legs up and around behind me. I was over the wall in just seconds and landed to the right of him at the bottom.

He just gave me a half-smile.

I gave him a quick nod, and we both turned toward our last obstacle, the military crawl. We approached the barbed-wire-lined mud pit together, and at the same time, we got on our stomachs to grind through the next three hundred feet.

By this week of the training, we had learned this was not the time to slow down just because we were almost done and lying on our stomachs. Instead, the trick was to push harder to finish strong.

We pressed the insides of our feet into the ground and rotated our knees out so our hips hugged the mud as closely as possible. As we moved in sync under the sharp tips of the barbed wire, he would sneak a glance from the corner of his eye and meet mine, and I would give him a smirk. This was a ridiculous way to connect with a hot guy, but there I was, covered in mud and feeling flush. We reached the end of the obstacle at the same time and emerged together from the muddy pit.

"That was impressive..." He searched for my name on my uniform. I used the back of my sleeve to wipe off the mud. "Moreno."

"Yeah, that was my fastest time yet." I looked at my watch, but really I was taking a moment to breathe as I realized what I had done. The dark mist gave me some kind of supernatural strength. But at what cost? Everything had a cost.

"Let's get some lunch. My treat," Baine said.

"It's a date."

We washed our hands at the cleaning station nearby and grabbed an MRE, a Snickers and a Gatorade from the table set up at the course entrance. He and I were among the first of the recruits to complete the course, which gave us more downtime than the others, considering that ninety percent of our flight was still out there. There were plenty of logs and benches neatly lined up, giving us a more suitable place to enjoy all the fine dining that the MREs didn't offer. The food might be horrible, but the seating was an upgrade from the floor.

Now that the race was over I observed his aura. I wanted to know if it would flash red then purple again, and in fact, it did.

Trust your instincts, Sasha. This was something I repeated to myself a lot, because the alternative would be believing this was all just one big, convoluted delusion, and that just wasn't an option for me right now. I had come too far just to doubt myself. Funny how being in the presence of this model of a chiseled sun god would bring up my insecurities again.

"So, what's today's mystery meat?" I picked up the aluminum bag and searched the side for the description.

"Chicken marsala." He grimaced.

"Ok, you're not selling it to me." I laughed. "I don't know why, but right now I'm craving a pot roast."

"My mom makes a killer pot roast." He smiled, but it quickly disappeared.

"I bet you can't wait to take leave and have it again." I was searching—for what, I still didn't know.

"Yeah," he said softly.

"I'm Sasha, by the way." I held out my hand.

"I'm Trent."

I felt an electric charge as soon as he took hold and fought the urge to snap my hand back. He was silent as he finished the rest of his meal-in-a-wrapper. I poured some into my mouth and picked up my Gatorade. I took a sip to wash down the aftertaste of vacuum-sealed processed meat.

Trent Baine. I committed it to memory as though the explanation for our connection lay somewhere in a name.

More recruits finished the course and started to sit on the logs around us. Santos was among them; she looked over at me and winked when she saw me chatting up Mr. Sunshine. I winked back and wondered how I was going to get Baine to tell me more about his mother without sounding pushy or annoying.

"Well, my mother has never made a pot roast, but she makes a mean carne asada." I licked my lips at the thought of it.

"That sounds good. I don't think I've ever had carne asada."

I smiled at the funny way he pronounced those two words. He didn't return my smile. I was losing him. I focused in on his red aura and sent mine out wider to merge with his. I wanted him to feel like he could trust me.

"Sorry, it's just... my mother is fighting cancer," he said. "She has been for years. I almost didn't join because I didn't want to miss any time with her, but here I am."

I was in awe of my newfound ability, if it even was an ability. I mean, was he telling me this because I'd joined my energy with his just now, or was he naturally opening up to me?

"I totally get it." I sighed, recalling all those visions I'd had recently. Baine's dying mother, Grange and his festival of orgies... "I've been struggling with something of my own."

"What do you mean?"

I couldn't believe I'd just said that. I must've been too caught up in his energy. It felt safe, like I could tell him things. But there was no way I could tell him this crazy shit going on with the TI... or could I?

Chapter 18

I eased my energy from his, not wanting to expose him to the corruption I knew existed inside me.

Guilt washed over me. He'd probably think I'd brought this all on myself. He certainly wouldn't believe the TI was an actual monster.

Just when I was trying to pull myself together, I looked back into his eyes. He looked like a combination of a comforting sunrise in the morning with the smell of warm muffins in the oven. Baine had both a hot and approachable vibe, all at the same time. I caved.

"Well, there's a certain TI who harasses me and some of the other recruits in the female dorm. He threatens to plant things like cocaine and knives in our personal belongings." I left out the part about how all the girls in the dorm were mesmerized by him.

Since our energies were still partially woven together, I felt a black shockwave of rejection flash outward from his center. I slowly transitioned my energy to white to offset the inner turmoil within him, and to my surprise, he received the white and allowed himself to be wrapped in it. His face went from having a wrinkled brow to a softened forehead. He raised his hand over his mouth, considering me.

"Whoa, that's intense. Sorry you have to deal with an asshole like that," he said, shaking his head. "I have this one TI who's an extreme bitch. We all figure she's overcompensating because she's a female. She makes our days hell. But the guy TI is all right."

"Thanks. I just wish there were a way to stop him," I said. "Some way to bust him for good. I thought if I had a video camera or a voice recorder, we could record him while he's saying all these perverted things to us. We know the other TIs won't believe us. I just don't know what else to do."

"Yeah, there's no way to get any of that kind of stuff in here," he said, taking a huge bite of his Snickers bar.

"So, you actually do like Snickers?" I asked as a piece of the caramel filling lay gently across his lip. He licked it off before I could say anything.

"Oh." He laughed and looked at the bar in his hand. "I love them. It just looked like you really wanted another one that day."

Watching us like this, both of us covered in a blanket of white, gave me a lot of insight into Baine's character. He had to possess white energy in order to merge with mine. All I was doing was enhancing what was already inherent within him. That was both fascinating and soothing, especially when we were talking about a potential vampire who preyed upon the lust of my dorm mates.

"Five minutes!" we heard a TI yell in the distance.

"Listen, don't let that TI get away with it," he said, standing up. "Don't do anything he says, and if you have to, kick him in the balls,"

"I will," I said. For once, I didn't feel so alone in all my confusion.

We marched in formation with sweaty uniforms caked in mud. I tried to keep my mind focused on the achievements of the day and the countdown to graduation, but my mind drifted back to Baine. When would I see him again? Would he be getting the news about his mom tonight or tomorrow?

I thought it had to be tonight because it was Monday. That would give him Tuesday, Wednesday and some of Thursday back home before returning to base by Friday like the TI had said in my meditation. This was assuming my visions were real. But it could still happen tomorrow night, and he would have a full day and a half at home. Since that would be so much more of a coincidence, I was very curious to find out if my ability was valid.

TI Grange called out cadence, snapping me back to the moment. "Your left! Your right. Your left! Your riiiight..."

Hearing his voice reminded me about his role in all this. I sent up a silent prayer he would leave us alone forever. But I knew that was unlikely. If my vision manifested, then I hoped this would all unfold after Baine was back from visiting his mom. And while I was sending out prayers, I thought, *Please, Baine, bring me back a recording device.*

After such an intense day on the obstacle course, I fell asleep on my cot the second I hit the sheets. I tried to get to the goat shed and meditate my way into Baine's energy field, but my body and mind were not having it. I awoke the next morning with my muscles sore from the previous day. Exhausted, I still searched for Baine, the very first thing at formation.

Since everyone was in uniform, I had to search for subtle differences in height, weight, hair and skin colors, and shapes of heads. It was incredible how quickly the human mind could adapt and detect even the smallest details.

We marched from the dorms to the dining hall, and I still hadn't seen Baine. In formation, we couldn't turn our heads and look around freely like a civilian would, so in my impatience, I tried to feel his energy. We arrived at the dining hall and lined up to get our trays. I couldn't find him with any of my senses.

"There's no maître d' here, Beauty Queen," the TI slurred from behind me. The heat from his breath along the back of my neck shot a series of warm tremors through my body. "Looking for someone?"

Shit. I froze in place, not wanting to begin the battle between my body and my mind today. My hands grew even hotter and sizzled under my tray. *What's up with all this heat in my hands?*

"At ease. Get your breakfast," he said, turning away from me. Someone else caught his attention across the hall, and he decided to go torment them instead.

The day continued like this. I searched for Baine and couldn't find him. At weapons training, I saw the dorm guard who'd spoken to Baine in my vision. There was a space at the table next to him, so I brought my weapon over to it to inspect and assemble before qualification practice.

"Hey," I said as I set my things down.

He gave me a blank look. Of course—this was the first time I had spoken to him in the six weeks we'd been there. "Uh, hey."

I wasn't sure how I was going to get him to tell me anything, so I figured it couldn't hurt to just come right out and ask. "I haven't seen Baine today. Is something wrong?"

He blinked a few times and looked back down at his rifle. "He's dealing with a personal issue," he grunted under his breath.

I got the feeling he was trying to ignore me.

"Is it his mother? Is she ok?" I asked.

He looked up at me now and his shoulders relaxed, his eyes finally meeting mine. "Oh, yeah, so he told you about her. She might not make it through the night. He went home to visit her."

I found my breath and exhaled.

"But he said he could come back and still graduate with us if he made it back by Friday."

"It'll be rough for him today," I said. He seemed to love his mother.

I froze. My hands tightened around the rifle I was holding, and I forgot what to do next. I had disassembled and reassembled my weapon now a dozen times. Today we would be qualifying on these weapons and my mind was completely blank.

I must have freaked the dorm guard out, because he said, "Hey, you ok?"

"Oh, yeah. Thanks, yeah. I'm ok. I'm fine."

It had dawned on me that this was all real. I had the ability to see things beyond myself. To tell the future. And it wasn't speculation anymore; it was an absolute fact I'd just proven to myself. This wasn't like when Nikki's mom said I had "precognition abilities" after I told her about my dreams. Back then there wasn't enough proof. But now I knew she was right.

I needed something from Baine. I needed him to bring me that voice recorder. I was going to go back to my goat shed and meditate my ass off to get in contact with him. I needed to take down TI Grange.

The mechanical process of reassembling my weapon returned to me then, and I was ready to qualify.

Chapter 19

Spirits were high in the dorm that evening as we settled down for the night. The entire flight had qualified on our weapons and aced our academic exams, outperforming all other week-six flights. We'd achieved "exemplary performance," according to our TI. I thought about Trent and hoped he would get a chance to qualify on his weapon as soon as he was back.

Lights-out was supposed to be at 2100 hours, but it seemed they were giving us extra time to chat among ourselves and enjoy our accomplishments. Unlike the others, I resented the extra time because I wanted to get to my goat shed. Some of the other recruits tried to talk to me, but I brushed them off, in no mood for all this celebration. I had an agenda and was ready to get to it. Twenty long minutes later, lights were finally out, and I was already settled in my bed waiting for the hustle and bustle to end so I could get into zen mode.

It wasn't working. Ten minutes passed, and I couldn't find myself in the goat shed. I realized my shoulders were tense, and my face was all pinched up like I'd just eaten a lemon. I was still annoyed at the extra time they gave us, so I was taking even longer to get settled. I had to remember the rules governing the energetic field of my visions. I couldn't feel annoyed or happy. Not frustrated or attached to finding out anything about Trent.

I could have the intention of achieving a certain goal, but no expectation it would actually happen. By knowing my premonitions were in fact real, by being frustrated, I had set myself a huge expectation that I would learn something important by going into my realm tonight. All this overthinking was setting me up for failure.

Let's try this again.

I took three deep breaths and scanned my body from top to bottom just like Ms. Gabriel taught me. I acknowledged any sensations and any non-sensations. I thanked my body for all it did for me. I could see the thoughts passing through my mind.

There was the worried thought about what Trent was doing and the uncertainty about whether he would help me. The thought about the TI and whether he would try something with me again. Then about my family and whether my mother would be proud when I graduated. I had so many expectations and worries.

Ok, Sasha, time to detach from these thoughts so you can get into the VIP room in your mind. One by one, I visualized a string connecting each thought to me. I held a huge pair of scissors and used them to cut each string. As I cut the first thought, it scurried away like a ferret running into a bush. I cut the second thought, and this one floated off like a balloon into the sky. And so they all went, with me cutting strings of thoughts and the thoughts vanishing—poof—into the abyss from whence they came. My mind was now clear, and the VIP room awaited.

I opened my eyes within my lucid dream and saw the shed's peaceful white curtains swaying gently in the tropical breeze. *So Hum...* Here I was, staring out upon another evening with clouds painted gold, pink and purple over the green mountain range sprawled out before me. Palm trees rocked in the distance, and the ever-present coquis sang out all around.

It was easy to forget why I'd come and just sit there instead. For a while, I did just sit there and take it all in. If this was all there was, it would be enough. Then, after a few minutes, I heard a muffled cough and remembered I was not here, inside the goat shed. I was in a meditative state inside a dream, and I had something I needed to do.

I brought images of Baine to mind, but nothing happened. I couldn't see anything. Then I recalled the images I'd seen of him with his mother on his patio. I gave it a little more time, but that didn't work either. I decided I would retrace my steps from the night when I'd actually succeeded.

I took a dive in the still lake and swam around for a little while, working on thought detachment so I wouldn't rush the process and instead allow the thoughts to flow freely. I stepped out of the cool water onto the fern-covered soil and leaned over the water and look at my reflection.

I placed my large black paws firmly on the bank. There I was, droplets of water dripping from my glossy black hair that covered every inch of my body, surrounded by a red aura that shifted to purple. My green eyes glowed in the face of a black jaguar now. The nagual. Dang, I wished I could shift like this in real life. I focused on a mental image of Baine, and the moment my energy shifted to purple, I saw his reflection in the lake.

He was sitting by his mother's bedside, holding her hand. Her face was pale and wrinkled beyond her years. Half her head was shaved, and there were stitches on the side. Clear plastic tubes kept her alive for what were now surely her last minutes. There was no fuzz, no blur in the image the way I'd seen the premonition the other night. This was either happening right now or it had already happened. *How hard it must be for Baine, to not be able to be here for her.*

Now that I knew my vision about Baine's mother was true, I could expect that what'd happened with that vampire douche TI would also manifest. I felt for Baine, I really did, but I had a purpose here, and it was to make sure he brought me back a recorder. I searched around his energy field, trying not to cause a disturbance, but it was a mess in here. Lots of sorrow, hurt and frustration. He was angry at himself. It was hard to sift through these strong emotions and find anything that wasn't about his mother. They must have been very close.

I sensed tension in my body again and had to consciously let go. No attachments, I reminded myself. As he sat there, eyes filled with tears and fighting back a big ugly cry, I knew what to do. I shifted my energy to white and penetrated theirs.

She was easy to envelop; her aura was almost entirely gone anyway. Only a faint silver light glimmered from her skin. A normal aura surrounded a person up to about six inches out. As soon as the white merged with her silver, her face softened, and the corners of her mouth turned ever so slightly upward. She knew I was there.

On the other hand, Baine's aura glowed a fierce red and black. Lightning bolts of red sparks shot out from the center. His grief was full of anger, and it was so strong it rejected the white energy instantly. *Ok, so let him be.*

He had the right to be angry. It was like a hurricane within his energy field. I tried to search for blurry images, like the ones I suspected told the future, but I couldn't see anything except the rage.

I focused my energy back on his mother. The vibration of her energy got stronger when I returned, and I wondered how I would let her know who I was and what I was doing there. She was standing now, wearing a long white dress with her hair flowing as though she'd just come from a salon.

"So, I guess you know Trent from basic training?" she said.

So now I was seeing spirits? "Yeah... How did you know that?"

"I can see it. I can see a lot of things I never saw before," she said with a serene smile. "What is your name?"

"I'm Sasha," I said, feeling a bit rude for not introducing myself sooner. "Are you dead?"

"No, dear, but my time is close. I am ready," she said. Her energy extended out to mine, connecting with it like an electric blanket. Her warmth surrounded me.

"I know this might sound strange, but I wonder if you can help me," I said. "I need Trent to bring me back a recorder. It's really important."

"Well, it won't come as a surprise to you when I say I can see that. In the same way you see things."

My eyes opened wide and a hopeful smile crossed my lips. "So, you see things, too! Finally, I'm not alone in all of this. How does this work? Will you help me understand?"

"I don't know any more than you do, dear," she said, looking back at Trent. Her attention now focused on him. She wanted to get back to him.

I looked down, fidgeting with my hands. These two needed their time alone.

"Will you tell him to help me?" I asked. I couldn't believe I was asking a dying woman for her final act on Earth.

"I will, but for my own reasons as much as yours. I want him to go back and finish, and I don't think he will unless he has a good reason."

The colors holding her energy dissipated into nothing. On the bed, her head turned toward Trent, and she slowly opened her eyes.

When Trent noticed she was awake, his eyes softened, his expression lightened, and the blasts of rage stopped shooting from his core. "Hey, Mom."

"Hi, Bear," she replied in a scratchy, faint voice.

He picked up a cup of water from the table and placed the straw right at her mouth so she could take a drink.

"Honey, I'm ok. You shouldn't be here. You need to finish your training." She searched his face for agreement.

"Mom, I need to be here now," he said in one defeated breath.

"No. No, you don't. No matter what happens, you get on that plane, and you graduate, ok? It's what I want."

His forehead wrinkled in defiance, but he nodded slowly and placed his other hand on top of hers.

"Listen, I don't know how to tell you this, so I'm just going to come out and say it," she said, pausing so she could cough. "You have a friend in basic—her name is Sasha, I think—and she needs your help, ok? She needs you to bring her a voice recorder." She squeezed his hand tightly.

"What in the world are you talking about? How could you possibly know that?" he said, releasing her hands.

"Honey, it's hard to explain. I don't know how this works." She closed her eyes and tilted her head back with a grimace. "All I know is you have to help her. It's really important."

"I barely know her, and I could get in a lot of trouble. What, did she call you? This is nuts," he said, standing up and pacing.

"It's not nuts. You remember your Great-Aunt May? How she used to read the tarot cards and get them right every time? And how she could talk to your dead Uncle Stevie? This girl can do things like that. She knows you're here, and she came to ask me for your help. She's here now, by the way."

His face turned to stone. His lips parted, and his eyes widened. "What do you mean, she's here now?" He scanned the room.

"Her energy traveled here." Her voice was soft and strained.

I felt completely naked and exposed watching this conversation unfold. I was crazy two days ago, and now I was an energy-traveling psychic? Baine was probably going to hate me now for meddling with his mother. I was certainly crazy to think he would help me; I was nobody to him.

"She's incredible, Mom." He just blurted it out, as though it was just hitting him. "She beat all the guys on the obstacle course the other day; none of us could believe it. She caught up to me from way in the back. She's like GI Jane with hair. You'd like her."

I'd had no idea he'd even noticed.

"Oh, I do like her, Bear." Her voice started to fade.

His smile shifted into an intense stare as he sat back down in the chair, taking his mother's hand once again. He studied her, memorizing her, turning her hand in his and caressing the back of it gently.

"If you want me to help her, I'll play along. It all sounds loco to me, but I remember that time Aunt May asked Uncle Stevie how to reset the sprinkler system, and I watched her do it step by step." He laughed. "As bad as she was at everything mechanical, I knew Aunt May wasn't joking with me." He paused, then said, "Ok, Sasha, if you're listening"—he looked around the room—"I'm coming back to base tomorrow, and I will bring the voice recorder. Our code word is 'Bear.' Call me that when you see me, and I'll know this is all for real."

Chapter 20

"You all think you're ready for graduation next week?" TI Grange belted out as we lined up in formation on Tuesday of week seven.

The heat from the sun graced my back, and the air was fresh from a morning rain. As we prepared to head to combat training, I spotted the familiar red energy floating around Baine a few rows up from where I stood.

"Yes, sir!" we yelled in unison.

"Today, we're headed over to Combat Arms Training. All recruits will engage in hand-to-hand combat with pugil sticks. This is where I'll get to see if you're ready for the field. I expect all of you to hold your ground. Now, where are my road guards?"

I was the first of the four of us to run forward and stand in line at attention directly in front of the TI. The road guards were responsible for stopping traffic as the formation marched to the destination. I loved the rush of breaking out of the rows of recruits all lined up nice and neat. I also wanted to get a good warm-up before getting into combat. From the corner of my eye, I noticed Baine standing just to the right of me. Two road guards would take the back of the formation, and the other two would handle the front. I was relieved he and I would be the two at the rear.

"Ten-hut!" we heard the TI command. Everyone locked in at attention.

Over the past few days, I'd studied the depths of the TI's shadow, gathering whatever intelligence I could from the movements within the mist. I attempted to penetrate the shadow during the day by turning my own aura black with the darkest thoughts -the ones of my sadness and desperation after Omar's arrest.

This all required too much concentration, and whenever I tried, I'd be interrupted. There was also the risk that my practice would be exposed. There were simply no times during the day when I could just sit and meditate alone. There was always some place to go, some training to do and some people around. Lately, the TI was hovering more than usual, searching for the right opportunity to get me alone. Every time he got close to me, my body reacted in ways I couldn't control. The moist, wet heat would grow between my thighs, begging for his touch.

"Right face!"

The formation pivoted sharply to the right, and Baine and I took our positions as rear road guards. The TI yelled cadence and moved to the front of the formation.

"Welcome back," I whispered when the TI was out of earshot.

We were several feet from the back of the formation and far enough from the other recruits not to be overheard. I wanted desperately to say, "Welcome back, Bear," but the words wouldn't come out.

What if I said "Bear" and he didn't know what I was talking about? Would he think I was crazy? I wished I didn't have to bring him into any of this, but I really did need his help.

"Thanks," he said.

Even from across our formation I felt the TI looking at me. His gaze was intense and demanding, and most of me wanted that. My body craved his attention. I realized with the days of basic training coming to an end, I had to be ready. There was a finite amount of time left for him to make his move. I was surprised he hadn't tried already.

We marched on like this, blocking traffic as necessary as we headed to the training grounds. I wanted to blurt out "Bear" about five different times, but every time I tried, my throat tightened up as though rocks were stuffed inside.

When we arrived at combat training, Baine turned and looked me directly in the eye before we entered the building. His eyes were liquid blue with green speckles in the center, and he stared at me with a wildness, like an untamed animal that knew there was no way out. Tiny shocks of fury shot out from his core, and I could tell he was still hurting because he had to leave his mother.

In combat training, I was paired with Speed. Dressed in protective gear, we warmed up with our pugil sticks, taking light blows at each other until we were called to the center mats. When the TI announced for the first pair to begin, the whole room shot up with brightly-lit auras. We watched the a few other recruits spar, then it was our turn.

"You ready?" I asked, teeth clenched.

"Oh yeah, you're going down."

All signs of our friendship were gone, and all I saw was a warrior ready to pounce on me.

Her magenta glow shone even brighter. She stood a few inches taller than me at about five foot eight and weighed a good twenty pounds more than I did. She told me that back home she'd worked on the farm every day since she was little. Her muscles were refined over years of physical labor, and from what I could tell about her energy, she was sure she was going to take me down in a second.

"Start," yelled the TI.

I wasn't ready for her to slam right into me, pushing me back toward the edge of the circle. I planted my feet, but she was too strong. Any second I would fall out and lose points. I took a quick step right, but she was quicker, her stick landing heavy into my right shoulder. Pain shot through me, and I lost my footing. She slammed me again on my hurt shoulder, then again on my left. I couldn't get any blows in, and I just wanted to run. I stepped back five long paces to the far end of the circle, not taking my eyes off her for a second. Sweat dripped down my brow and back, my hands were clammy, and I was losing my grip on the stick.

But in those few seconds on the far end of the circle, I focused in on her aura. She moved her stick forward to the right of me, but before she did, her aura shot out in the same direction. Why hadn't I noticed this before? Next, she did the same thing on the left side, and the magenta glow moved to the left before she took a step. I responded with a weak push of my stick.

When Speed took a decisive step toward me on my right, her magenta glow shot out in front of her. I knew she'd come at me strong from that side, so I stepped left. Darkness crept into her aura. She was getting pissed, maybe even doubting herself. That was the darkness, the negative thought lingering within the person. She may've been my friend, but I had to learn about this new way I could use energy.

I quickly pulled the darkness into myself. The electric charge that had once scared the shit out of me turned into tornados. They seeped into me and rippled underneath my skin.

I repeated the little dance with Speed for a few steps; every time she came at me, I simply avoided contact. This bought me some time as the darkness consumed me.

We couldn't go on like this, and I could tell she was getting annoyed.

"What's wrong, Beauty Queen? Didn't they teach you how to fight in the pageants?" yelled TI Grange as he stood right behind me. He laughed.

Frowning, I leaned into my stance. The next time Speed came at me, I moved my stick to her opposite side and brought it hard into her right shoulder. Knocked off balance, she fell hard to the ground. She got back up after a few seconds, and when she did, she backed away from me. She seemed tired and worn out, but I wasn't.

"Halt," yelled the TI.

We left the sparring circle and took off our gear for the next cadets to use.

"I didn't expect that. You kicked my ass," Speed said as she removed her helmet, panting heavily.

"And here I thought you were just going easy on me." I laughed. Little did she know she would have had me if it wasn't for the way I'd fed off her energy.

I noticed Baine standing by the equipment bins and walked over. His was the only aura that wasn't bright with excitement; the rest of us relished the chance to take some stress out on each other. He was probably thinking about his mother and how she'd told him I'd basically eavesdropped on their conversation. It was now or never. I pushed past the awkwardness and went for it.

"Hey, Bear," I said, placing the helmet, harness and stick back in the bins.

His eyes softened, and he bowed his head for a second. Then he looked back up at me and blinked with acknowledgment of our code word. "Are you in on some kind of sick prank with my mom?" His mouth creased into a thin line, his eyes darkening.

I twisted my mouth and crossed my arms. "Of course not. Look, I know this is super weird. It's strange for me, too. But I need to know, are you going to help me?" My eyes shifted down and away from him. I stood at rest to his right so I wouldn't appear to be talking to him. Casual conversations in instructional spaces were completely off-limits.

"Yes, I have it." He gave me a side-eye up and down. "I'll bring it to you at dinner formation tonight."

A rush of energy shot up from my legs to my chest. That recorder was my insurance policy. "Did you remember to include batteries?"

He laughed, shaking his head. Finally, I got to see him smile. It sent a pulsing hum up through my core.

"Now, that would suck if I forgot," he said. "Lucky for you, I remembered."

That night, I held the voice recorder in my hand as I laid in my cot, ready to go to sleep. Baine had handed it to me before dinner, and I'd slid it in my cargo pocket. He said he'd no trouble sneaking it in. It was small enough to fit in the palm of my hand, silver and thin. I tested it out a few times, and it worked great.

He told me he'd hidden it in the lining of his suitcase, and a huge weight lifted off my shoulders when I knew he'd gotten away with it. The thought of him messing up his chances of completing his training—which was the one thing his mother wanted for him—wrung my nerves right out. I shook away that thought, grateful that that wasn't the case.

Chapter 21

Reveille sounded at 0445 hours, and I was still holding the recorder in my hand. I must've been exhausted, because I'd fallen right asleep without the chance to travel to the goat shed. Frustrated, I looked in the mirror as I tied my hair in a bun. It had grown a few inches since I'd cut it in week zero and was now out-of-regulation length. That wasn't the only thing that had changed. Something about my jaw line was firmer, something about my cheekbones more set and something about my eyes said I wasn't crazy. I finished getting dressed for PT.

Then I felt it. I could always feel it before I saw it. My mouth filled with the taste of metal, and I had the urge to scratch myself all over as a frigid chill shot down my spine. These were the signs of the mist at its worst. It was the start of week eight, and sometime this week I'd find out if I would become a SERE.

Everyone had left for morning PT except for Santos and me. We were told to stay behind because TI Grange wanted to issue our orders privately.

Dressed in our gray T-shirts and blue shorts, we both sat outside the TI's office, waiting to be called in. Santos looked over at me, a scream hidden behind her eyes. She knew exactly what he wanted with her, and I knew what he wanted with us both.

"Enter, Moreno."

Thank the stars these sweat shorts had pockets. Honestly, everything should just have pockets. I'd thought about putting the recorder between my breasts or securing it behind my bra strap, but I was worried he would grab me in one of those places before I had the chance to catch something incriminating. I had tested the sound recording quality from my pocket, and it was slightly muffled, but it worked. It would have to do.

I slid the button on the recorder to the "on" position. My body felt double my normal weight as I tried to stand up from the chair, and, when I tried to move my feet, it was like they were being held down by twenty-pound weights. I took a few painful steps forward and looked back at Santos for motivation. She wouldn't lift her gaze from the floor.

"We got this," I whispered to her before I walked into his office. I wasn't letting her give up. No way.

My stomach lurched at the sight of him sitting there with his paperwork in his hands. The mist of darkness surrounding him parted, opening a clear view of ominous perfection. I took a deep breath and approached his desk, my heartbeat pounding in my chest with every step.

"You're full of surprises, Beauty Queen." His voice was low and dark. "When this assignment came across my desk, I must say, I hesitated. The training is ten times tougher than boot camp. I worry about you and that hint of crazy I can tell you have behind those wild green eyes of yours. But then I looked at the bright side. We could see a lot more of each other, because the training starts right here at Lackland."

My face burned. I was hoping to be far away from him by the end of this week.

"So, you ready to know what it is?"

"Yes, sir."

"Ok, but first there's something you should know. It requires my recommendation. They need to know if I consider you physically and psychologically ready for the demands of this assignment. It's a good assignment. In my opinion, one of the best. The things you'll learn will prepare you for anything."

I tried not to flinch at what I knew was coming next. I stared at his mouth as it opened, willing myself to see the creature behind the mask. That's when I saw his two sharp fangs set inside of his mouth and the long tongue that ran over them. I must be seeing something that was hidden from people without my abilities.

"Enter, Santos!" he yelled out of nowhere.

Her energy was dim as she entered, and her face resembled a stone statue. She was probably trying to resist whatever power he had over her. I watched as her expression went from one of impending doom to eager anticipation. With just a look, she was under his spell.

"Now Moreno, I think Santos can help you understand something important. Santos, tell Moreno the magic word."

"Compliance," she said with a sensual smile and a little bounce.

"Yes, that's it. Compliance. What I want—no, what I need—is for you to comply. Like Santos has complied. This is how we all get what we want."

I swallowed what felt like a sparrow clinging to the lining of my throat, its sharp nails scratching as it went down. *Why do I want him so bad? Resist him, Sasha!*

"Come here and stand at attention."

I'd better do as he said or maybe he'd spank me like a bad little recruit. I pictured myself thrown over his lap, his hands smacking against my bottom and leaving a stinging red mark where it landed.

Agh! Focus!

He stood up from his desk, reached over and grabbed Santos's hand. She stepped closer, obviously wrapped up in his seductive trance as she placed her lips against his. Kissing him, she unbuttoned his shirt and moved her touch slowly down to his pants.

All the while, he stared into my eyes.

I returned the gaze, working really hard to focus on my anger, my rage. Those emotions were strong enough to overpower the lust hungering for his touch.

Santos unzipped his pants, revealing an impressively thick, firm erection.

"I-I can't do this," I forced out, remembering the recorder in my pocket and the need to get this all on record. "I don't want to."

"Now, that's fine. You don't have to. And I don't have to give you my recommendation," he said as Santos wrapped her hands around him.

"Santos, has he made you do this before?" My eyes pleaded with her to speak the truth even as I struggled against my own traitorous body. "Has he asked you to give him a blow job?"

"Well, he hasn't asked, but I know what he wants," she said.

But my words seemed to snap her out of whatever hypnotic sex coma she was in. Her hands grew slack. "He made me," she whispered, realizing she really didn't want to do this.

My hand clenched into a tight fist, so tight my knuckles turned white.

"Now, don't make me out to be such a bad guy, Santos. You came to me, remember?" His face was calm perfection even though his eyes darkened.

"No, no, I don't want this." She let go of him and moved backward.

It took all my energy to push his control over my sexual desires aside and only focus on the rage. The rage outpaced the lust, and I drew the dark mist into me again. There was a counterpull this time, something like pulling a magnet off a piece of metal, and in this case, Grange was the metal.

He was pulling the shadows, too.

But I had the element of surprise. I don't think he expected me to have a similar ability. I drew the darkness into me once again, and a fire rose in my chest and through my hands.

The heat was out of control. On instinct, I put my hand next to his crotch and opened my fist. A blazing fire released from my hand, scorching his flesh for one quick second. It was all I needed.

He screamed, curling over his body and falling to his chair. I linked my arm with Santos's and pulled her up. She stumbled backward, and I had to steady her.

Did I just shoot fire from my freakin' hand? Just like in my dreams! I had to figure out how I'd done that.

We stood as he twisted in pain in his chair. His tongue slithered out of his mouth, unnaturally long and pointed sharply at the end. He bared his fangs at us with a hiss. A dark mist spun off of him into a bunch of tornados, wringing out a high-pitched squeal.

I shook out my hand, the sting of the fire reverberating through my skin, and then I slid it into my pocket, making sure the recorder was still there.

Santos looked over at me with desperation in her eyes, shaking her head. "Oh no, oh no, oh no."

"Ha, Moreno. What are you?" Grange choked out as he tried to regain his composure. He stood up slowly. "I knew you weren't like the others. I could taste it on you."

"What does that mean?" Santos demanded, her eyebrows perked up and her eyes moving from him to me and back again.

The TI flicked his wrist, and her expression returned to one of simple concern.

"Sir, I had nothing to do with this, ok?" Santos gasped after what felt like a moment of stunned silence. "I can't get kicked out."

Did he just cast some sort of spell on her? What was that he did with his wrist?

"Can't you see what he is?" My heart pounded in my chest.

"What? No. I don't know what I just saw." She shook her head. "Everything is so confusing."

"Not only won't you be getting your orders," Grange said, "but you'll both be kicked out for insubordination."

His face was no longer contorted with pain. His shadow tornados were no longer spinning around him; they'd regrouped behind him, small and contained. I had never seen his shadow so meek. I saw the faint glow of a blue aura lingering around. I would have expected the opposite—that it would grow with fury.

My thumb touched the cool silver metal of the recorder in my pocket as I figured out what to do next. I could replay the recording right then and there. Santos would know I had him. He'd know he was screwed, that I had it all on audio.

I wanted him to know—so badly—it was his career that was over, not ours. But I couldn't do that. He'd do whatever it took to take this recorder from me. No, I had to get away from him and share this with someone I could trust.

"You've been harassing Santos and me since the beginning. I don't know how many times you've had Santos in here, but I know you've been harassing me since the start. How many women have you preyed on over the years? Dozens? Hundreds? You've got this whole routine down, manipulating us, threatening us with drugs and weapons. But I know exactly the kind of monster you are, and I am telling you this has to stop. Right. Now!"

I'd yelled that last bit, hoping someone would hear us. But we were still all alone in the dorm. None of the others had returned. Time was slower now. The clock above his desk had stopped moving, and the walls began to warp.

"There's something I think you're having trouble with, Moreno, and that's acceptance," Grange said. "You need to accept this is the way we do things around here. All the other girls before—and yes, there have been many—knew what they needed to do to get what they wanted. I helped them get their assignments. They were happy to let me take care of them, like I would've taken care of Santos. This is how things work around here, and you, well, you'll just crawl back into the little hole where you came from." He flicked his fingers as though he was swatting away a fly.

There was a rumbling, and the dark shadows around him caved into itself. Then it burst forth, the darkness slithering out of his arms, chest and legs like snakes. They started small, insignificant, then grew in both size and shape.

The deepest parts of the Shadow were as dark as midnight and only I could hear the shrieks within. The Shadow spoke with a husky tone. "Now you are under arrest for assault and battery of your superior. You will be court martialed, and with Santos's testimony, convicted of a felony," he said, his words echoing in the dark energy field surrounding him.

"Santos, don't do it. It's going to be all right. We can get through this together," I pleaded as the recorder burned with the desire to be free of my hot and stuffy pocket.

Santos looked down at her hands, fidgeting. Tiny beads of sweat formed at the very top of her forehead.

"That's right. Santos is a witness to you assaulting me when I wouldn't recommend you for SERE training." Grange stood even taller and moved toward the phone. He picked up the receiver, placed it against his ear and dialed.

The room became devoid of air, and my chest pulsed as I tried to find my breath. I watched in awe as his darkness condensed tightly back into him as he spoke on the phone. Its presence was almost entirely diminished while his face and features returned to his normal cool and commanding presence.

Chapter 22

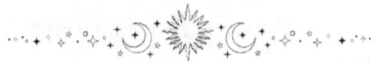

I barely had time to acknowledge the news about the SERE training assignment when the security police arrived to take me away. It was the assignment I had wanted, the future I'd dreamed of, and now it was fading before my eyes.

The military police pushed me up against the wall like an armed criminal and patted me down. Just like I expected, they found nothing in my pockets or on my body. Good thing I still had a quick mind about me. The police slapped some handcuffs on me, and I was escorted out of the dorm just minutes after all the others had arrived.

My eyes stung as I was being arrested. It felt like a chemical, my eyes tearing like they did whenever I got too close to a campfire. I bowed my head and squinted my eyes as I was escorted out, unable to look or read the others' faces.

This didn't feel vindicating and empowering like the night I'd confronted the not-TI shadow form at El Morro. No, this felt like something entirely different. There was a monster in that office, and I was the one in handcuffs being taken away. Well, there went my hopes and dreams of making something of my life.

The TI walked behind us, his footsteps clamoring on the floor along with the others. When we reached the downstairs patio, I felt a blast of fresh air on my face. It helped me open my eyes again. Grange was speaking to one of the sergeants a few feet away and out of earshot.

"He's lying. Whatever he is saying, he's lying!" I yelled as the officer tightened his grip.

"That's enough," he said.

Grange gave me a cold stare as the security police shoved me into the vehicle.

"Looks like you'll be headed to the brig soon," said the driver. His voice was light and peppy. "That's where they send all the female prisoners, especially once the JAG gets ahold of ya."

I stared blankly out the window and realized from this point on, I had no control over what would happen.

For several hours I sat in a box of a room with worn white bricks enclosed by a metal door. The room had a grim wooden bench with initials and illegible words carved by what I assumed were fingernails. The silence was the only thing about the room I found refreshing—no, it was invigorating. In this room, I couldn't hear the constant hum of the Shadow's whispers or see the torment it wished to bring upon me.

All I had were my thoughts, and I had gotten good at slowing those down.

You're crazy. You just got yourself kicked out of here.

Another thought came tumbling in. *You thought all this happened for a reason. You actually thought you went through this deep, trying time in your life to lead you right here. Did you really think you could get your life together? Find some magical shaman? Become a nagual? The joke's on you. The truth is, all you are is crazy and destructive, and nothing about you ever mattered.*

No. Think! I screamed at myself. That thing was a blood-sucking vampire, a real-life vampire. I had visions, I could see the future and even influence it. I'd proved that with Baine. And in such a vision, I saw a beast take over the body of a younger version of Grange. Was I the only human on this earth who could see these creatures?

Just then, I slapped my palm against my forehead. This is what the shadow dreams meant by training. I wasn't alone; there were others, and there was even a training school for people like me. I needed to find it. But how could I do that when I was here, locked away?

I shot up and began to pace.

The growing rage inside me didn't want to be calmed. I wanted to be upset with the TI for all he had done and with myself for not telling the police about the recorder when I'd had the chance. The rage within demanded I fight. I had to get out of here so I could find the missing shaman.

I focused on the rage, the anger, the frustration building in me once again, and felt my hands fill with the fury of it all. All of these emotions coursed through my body, collecting at my palms, and a small fire ignited there once again.

The heat startled me, and I closed my palms on instinct. I could really do this. I could fucking summon fire! Now, if only I could do one big enough to blast through that door.

I tried again... Nothing. Then I tried again, and nothing.

"Agh!" I yelled in frustration. I banged my fist against the door and pressed my forehead against the cool wooden surface.

I needed to rest my mind from so much emotional and mental focus. I sat on the bench with my legs crossed, my eyes closed and my hands open on my thighs. I tried to meditate, yet I couldn't get to the place of nothingness. There was zero chance I could access that serene VIP room of my mind.

My T-shirt suddenly became itchy, the pits damp with sweat, and my hands clammy. I imagined myself in front of the commanding officer when they started to question me.

Let's see, sir, I regularly see dark, ominous shadows around everyone, especially the TI. If I squint my eyes, I can even see demonic creatures and dead people in those shadows.

I would go on to tell the commander that this is how I knew Grange was a vampire. That I knew the guy was bad news when I dream-walked into his sick mind and saw a beast take over his body, and he fantasized about Santos and me in lacy lingerie under his desk. Then I got a fellow recruit to bring me a voice recorder by talking to his dying mother's spirit, just so that I could expose the TI for the paranormal beast he really is.

I laughed out loud—that kind of wild, unbelievable laugh when you see a magician doing tricks on amateur night. This would all sound perfectly believable to the commanding officer who'd then ask me for the voice recorder, and I would tell him I didn't have it. I would be committed to an insane asylum for the rest of my life and required by law to take psychiatric meds that turned me into a zombie.

My knees met my chest and I curled into myself on the hard wooden bench.

Chapter 23

"Moreno." I barely heard the call after I'd drifted into a fitful sleep with my back against the hard brick wall.

I lifted my head slowly, blinking. Within seconds, the security police at the door came into focus.

"The commanding officer will see you now," he said.

I uncurled my body and stood, unprepared to make a case or have anything compelling to say. I was escorted into a plain room with several chairs around a dark metal table, and a large rectangular mirror loomed on the wall to my right. I was told to sit, and there I waited. This was an interrogation room. I recognized it from television shows.

As I drummed my fingers on the table, the door swung open, and a woman about my height walked in. She had short brown hair trimmed tightly around her ears and toward the back. It was longer at the top so her straight bangs could be whisked up so as not to cover her eyes. Her dress blues were crisp and impeccable. Judging from the faint wrinkles around her brown eyes, I guessed she was in her fifties. She held a stern gaze and entered without speaking. This cut my daydreaming short, and when I noticed her rank, I stood at attention and gave a stiff salute.

"At ease," she said.

She took a seat. The way she walked, sat with precision and gestured for me to sit down demonstrated decades of military conditioning and discipline. I, in comparison, must've appeared unremarkable and a mess sitting across the table from her.

I swallowed another sparrow as I considered my fate in the hands of this decorated colonel. To think I could meditate my mental imbalance away and create a fulfilling life for myself seemed completely absurd at this point.

"Recruit Sasha Moreno," she read from the paper in front of her. "I'm Colonel van Holst and the commanding officer of the Security Forces. You are now under my command, Moreno, and I am responsible for you."

All this time I'd assumed the colonel was a man, not a woman. Damn. Shame on me.

I nodded slightly, searching around her for a sign of the Shadow. Her energy glowed deep indigo and green, but there was no Shadow to be found. I exhaled for the first time in what felt like hours.

"How are you? Have they been treating you well?" she asked.

"Yes, ma'am." Why did she even care if I was ok if she was about to send me to the brig?

"First of all, let me start by saying there are a good number of personnel investigating this case right now," she said. "We have made it our top priority to understand what exactly happened."

I nodded robotically, because that was what was expected of me. Everything felt numb now. Even the tips of my fingers that lay flat on my thighs had lost sensation.

"So, I understand you found the recorder on his desk and turned it on while he wasn't paying attention, correct?"

I didn't know what the hell she was talking about. Wait... did she just come up with a cover for me? "Uh-huh."

"Lucky for you. Now I will ensure that part of the story remains confidential for the time being, considering all the circumstances."

I was still numb, nodding, unable to understand why she would bother covering for me.

"Your bravery in this situation is remarkable." She leaned in, placing her elbows on the table. "I've got to tell you, you're not alone. I know what you're going through."

She searched my eyes, and when she did, she snapped me out of my cerebral coma. Did she understand everything? Nah. No way.

"In my position, I've seen this kind of thing happen way too many times," she continued. "Sexual assault, like what happened to you and Santos, is incredibly hard to convict because of the burden of proof. With this recording, and Santos's testimony, we were able to immediately arrest MTI Grange and press charges."

Now would be a good time to tell her he was a vampire. I mean, she said she understood.

Too soon, Sasha. I shook the thought away.

The colonel sat back in her chair almost unnoticeably as she relaxed her shoulders and tilted her head to the right ever so slightly.

As soon as the colonel had finished talking, the silence in the room pounded in my ears. I was frozen, staring at her with wide eyes, mouth agape. Relief, anger, fear and frustration rushed to the surface at once. My eyes teared, and the salty drops spilled out without my permission. No doubt she'd see me weak with emotion when I should be proud and vindicated.

"It's ok. I get it. I brought these." She handed me a small pocket pack of tissues.

I wiped my tears away before meeting her eyes once again.

She laid the back of her right hand on the table now, the palm up. "There, take my hand, please. It really is ok."

I placed my hand in hers, and as I did, I was able to lift my head a little higher "I-I can't believe it. It's over?"

"Yes."

I felt full for what felt like the first time in my life. It was as though my heart had been sliced in five different pieces before this moment, and now each piece was joining together, whole again within my chest.

"I understand you are assigned to SERE training," the colonel said.

"Yes, ma'am."

"Good. The first fifteen days of the year-long training will be held right here. After reviewing your entrance exam, basic training test scores and overall physical performance, I think you're an excellent candidate for this program and will ensure you receive my recommendation."

I did my best to control the exaggerated smile that wanted to spread across my face and made sure she only saw a normal-sized professional one.

"If you're interested, I'd like to mentor you in this start of your military career. I believe I can help you, and from the looks of things, maybe you can help me, too."

"Yeah. I mean yes ma'am. I'm interested." I said, cocking my head to the side.

The past twenty-four hours had been an emotional roller coaster full of my own self-doubt and just trying to do the right thing. This would be the start of my career, and that scumbag demon TI Grange would be locked up where he belonged.

Relief swept over me as I realized I didn't have to look my mother in the face and tell her I'd messed up once again. I had a career now. I couldn't believe a broke girl from the hood with daddy issues could have come this far in such a short time. And as soon as the military gave me access to a computer, I'd begin my search for the shaman.

For now, I wanted some time alone to settle my nerves and calm my excited mind.

"Ok, recruit," the colonel said as if reading my mind, "we're just going to take your statement, and then you can join me in my office where I will personally ensure we both get some lunch. Then we'll figure out when you can get back to the dorms and reintegrated into the squadron. You've got work to do."

Though her posture remained stiff and unmoving, she flashed me a warm smile.

"Thank you, Colonel. But there is something I really need to know. What's going to happen to TI Grange?" I asked.

She shifted in her chair and interlaced her hands on the table in front of her. "He will face multiple charges of sexual assault with the judge advocate general. This is a developing investigation, and we will go through due process of interviewing all possible witnesses, collecting evidence, and interrogating TI Grange. With everything in order, he could be court martialed, stripped of his rank, pension and pay, and prosecuted for up to thirty years in military prison."

I wanted him castrated, but this would have to do.

Before I gave my statement, I asked her for the favor of speaking to Santos in private. She agreed. In my statement, I omitted any mention of vampires, auras, energy, the goat shed, the Shadow, Baine, the recorder or my lucid dreams.

"Thank you again, ma'am, for everything," I said.

"You're welcome, Moreno," she said with a brisk nod.

Before she stood up and saluted me, her aura flashed bright green, and I caught the slightest glimmer in her eyes, much like the one Nikki and I shared when we were up to something.

Wait, did she know something more? The glimmer vanished so quickly I wasn't even sure I'd actually seen it.

I saluted her with a stiff, proud arm. She returned the salute, pivoted sharply and left the interrogation room.

Overwhelmed, I tried to make sense of recent events, but it was still a jumbled mess. During my statement, instead of giving her all the facts, I told her only the facts that applied to the accepted, shared view of our physical world. I realized my view of the world was fundamentally different than everyone else's, and that might not necessarily be such a bad thing.

Chapter 24

My thoughts turned to Santos and the recorder. When TI Grange had been on the phone with the police, I'd grasped both her hands in mine. At my touch, it felt as though all the strength was drained from her body. I tried to meet her gaze, but she wouldn't look at me. As I pressed the smooth metal recorder to the inside of her palm, she raised her eyes to meet mine.

"Hey... remember Benny. You did the right thing. Listen to this," I whispered quickly, "then take it to the TI of our brother flight, Sergeant Smith. I believe he'll help you."

During our daily drills and classes, sometimes the TI of our brother flight would take over. It was a shared responsibility among the TIs, and they never told us who to expect. I sensed I could trust TI Smith based on the way he'd treated Baine when he'd had to go home. His energy felt honest.

Santos pulled her hands away along with the recorder. She slid it into her left pocket as she tightened her lips and stared blankly at the wall in front of her. If I just went off her expression, I wouldn't have been able to read her. But her aura turned a vibrant blue.

At the time, the vivid color hadn't been enough for me to hope that she would put herself at risk to follow through. She held my future in her hands, and up until an hour ago, I'd had no idea what she would do with it.

The door to the interrogation room opened slowly, and Santos stood in the doorway. Her blue aura was still radiant and to me, that made her seem bright with possibility. She stepped toward me and smiled. I returned the smile.

Ironically, the military had just the right slang for this moment.

"Yoooo, your fangs are out!"

"No, yours are." She laughed and joined my open embrace. We wrapped our arms around each other and squeezed tightly.

She stepped back and looked at me. "That was amazing, Moreno. I can't believe we got that asshat."

"We did."

"I saw him come in while I was in the waiting room," she said. "He was completely calm, even smug with himself. It creeped me out. And honestly, I still feel guilty. I hate to admit it, Sasha, but even after all that's happened, I still find him sexy as hell." She shook her head in disbelief. "I hate myself for what I still feel, and for what I did to Benny."

"Grange just so happens to have the genes of a god, and he knows it. It's not your fault he's a master at manipulating women. He threatened us both, and he deserves to go down. You heard what he said. He's done this to dozens, and you know he won't stop." My jaw clenched.

It just occurred to me that our prison and legal system couldn't hold a beast like him. He could probably take down the guards with his vampire strength. Then what? Would he come after me and Santos?

I shook the thought away. One battle at a time.

"Ok, so tell me, how did you do it?" Santos asked. "How did you get the recorder? How did you know when to have it with you? That was FM." FM was slang for *fucking magic*.

"It was all FM. Let's not talk about the recorder, ok?" I looked around the room with the subtleness of a baseball catcher at the plate. "So, what's your assignment? Where are you going after this?"

"I'm going to do exactly what I came in here for—Cyber Systems Operations." She placed her hands on her hips. "My boyfriend was assigned the same."

"That's an amazing assignment!"

She nodded and shoved me lightly in the shoulder. "By the way, you got a thing for Baine?"

"Umm, no. What are you talking about?"

"I can tell when people are crushing on each other. He was standing right next to the TI when I asked to talk to him privately. You know how the TIs are, always short and impatient with us. So, I had to show him the recorder so he would take me seriously and give me the time. Baine saw it, and you should have seen his face. It was like he'd seen a ghost."

"And... what happened?" I worked hard to keep my face from flushing red.

"Well, the TI told me to give him a minute, and Baine started asking me questions about you. Like where were you, why weren't you in the drills, what happened. Yo, he was seriously concerned. I told him I couldn't talk about it and that I was trying to get you out of serious trouble. Then when the TI came back and pulled me away, he insisted he come with me. He heard the whole thing."

My eyes must've given me away, because she gave me a sideways, knowing smile.

"Oh, hello, you two are hot for each other. I can tell," she joked.

"Whatever. He's nice."

"And nice to look at."

"Yeah, that, too."

ONE WEEK LATER

The sun was a glowing mandarin in the sky, and the clouds decided not to make an appearance. We felt a cool breeze blow from the west as we kept cadence with one another on our graduation run. My mother was there in the stands, waving. Lola stood out in the crowd with her thick black hair, slim figure and bright-red lipstick.

I couldn't wave back, but I was sure she didn't expect me to. She gave me a bright smile. I'd been curious all this time if she'd have the same red aura I remembered seeing as a young girl. When I saw her in the stands, it shone flame-red, just like her personality.

As our squad ran around the field holding our flags, I still couldn't believe I'd gotten this far.

Many times, I wondered if the world spoke differently to all of us. If what I considered to be the absolute truth of anything I saw or experienced could be completely different than what someone else considered to be true. I wondered if my life and the way I saw the world, no matter how strange and twisted, was not a defect, a mistake or a mental disability, but a gift.

A gift that allowed me to help not only myself but others, too. Others like Santos and all the future women Grange would've assaulted if we hadn't stopped him. With the new measures that Colonel van Holst planned to implement, we'd probably helped even thousands more.

After our run, we returned to the dorms to change into dress blues. We received our certificates on the grassy field and were joined by our family members afterward.

My mother ran up to me and gave me a big hug. "My girl, I am so proud of you!"

"Thank you," I said, returning her smile.

As we walked off the field, I noticed Trent's energy to the right of mine.

"Congratulations on being the honor graduate," he said.

"Thank you. Congratulations to you for being the male honor graduate," I chuckled and soft-punched his shoulder.

"I'd like to take these two honor graduate families out for dinner," said Baine's father, beaming.

A surge of electricity jolted through my entire body. So, this is what it felt like to do something right for once. I let that feeling sink in.

"Sounds good," I said. "Maybe this time our food will be served on plates. I'll make sure to get you a Snickers, too." I loved that we could laugh about this now.

"Oh, now you're talking," Baine said, standing closer than he ever had in the past.

For the first time in eight weeks, we were officially off duty. In a few minutes, we'd be driving out of the base gates for lunch in the downtown. And in a matter of days, Baine and I would begin SERE training. Our lives would never be the same.

I turned my attention to the bleachers and found Colonel van Holst standing there, staring at me with a serious expression on her face.

"Guys, give me a few minutes, ok? I'll meet you at the pavilion."

I walked toward her. After we exchanged salutes, she had the same calculating expression on her face I'd seen in the interrogation room.

She got straight to it. "I thought you'd like to know what happened to TI Grange."

"Yes, ma'am."

"He was sent to the Joint Zodiac Command. He's being processed now and will be transferred to his zodiac house for the hearing. For him to get the maximum sentence, you'll need to be called as a witness. You can only be called as a witness if you've found your shaman and have entered Zol Stria by the time of the hearing. And without your testimony, he will most likely be set free in Zol Stria. But don't worry, his access to Earth has been revoked for eternity."

I knew those organizations she'd mentioned didn't exist in this world. She knew everything...

But all I could do was stutter, "Um... Zol Stria? Ha... what?"

"I don't want to have to report to the Zodiac Command that you're slow to pick up things." All the compassion from our last conversation was gone. Impatience tainted her voice.

"I'm not slow." My fingers prickled with heat. *No one calls me slow.* I realized now I didn't really like her.

"I hope not." She looked me up and down. "Thanks to me, the Zodiac Command is currently evaluating your case and giving you an extension to joining Zol Stria's Aries Academy. They'd previously discarded your file and had forgotten about you.

"Something about this whole thing with Grange seemed off, so I dug a little deeper. I ran a correlation between your birthdate and your birth location in the Joint Zodiac database, and you were a direct match for being a nagual. I don't know how you even made it this far into your Transit of the Twelfth House without going psycho, but here we are."

She regarded me now, as if in wonder.

"But you are falling behind your faction, and that just won't do," she said. "I've put in a good word for you because of how skillfully you took down Grange. Besides, your military training here makes you a unique asset for our Joint Forces.

Grange is a young vampire. Someone converted him on this side of the Gate about twenty years ago, and we believe he's either part of an organization called the Dark Zodiac or he altered his abilities through the Dark Code they provided."

Although it was a lot of information to take in, I was just glad I was figuring some of it out.

"Our intelligence has picked up some paranormal frequencies in the Sierra Nevada de Santa Marta mountain range of Colombia. We believe your shaman is there. I'll ensure your team gets stationed nearby to give you a chance to track him down."

"Wait, hold on. I need to understand something."

The colonel eyed me impatiently.

"How is it that you have other nagual in the program, and I got lost in the system like this?" I asked. "I mean, how did you find them and not me?"

"It's not an exact science. Naguals are given their Soul Contracts before birth, and like I just said, their births align to the constellations at the time and location of their birth. However, there can be a hundred babies born on a given day at about the same time within a short distance of each other. And there can be only one nagual among them.

"Their traits manifest by their tenth birthdays, and we have our teams search out the most gifted, intelligent, athletic and paranormal children born within those coordinates. You slipped past our radar entirely because your shaman never reported in, and your abilities were never detected by our reconnaissance teams."

I understood now. I'd suppressed my gifts the moment Titi Lily died.

"Your shaman is bound to you. Each nagual is assigned a shaman along with their Soul Contract. Consider them like a case worker. They evaluate each case and make the recommendation into the program. Your shaman has been AWOL since before you were ten."

My eyes narrowed and my mouth fell into a thin line. "What are the Gates? What is Zol Stria?" This was all so confusing, and it was starting to piss me off how my life was just another roll of the dice for them.

"You ready?" my mother asked from behind me.

I wiped the confusion off my face as I turned to her.

"Yes, she's ready. I didn't mean to keep her," van Holst replied, smiling now and swiftly turning to walk away. "Wait, Colonel. I have more questions," I protested.

She turned back to me with what appeared to be an intentional resting bitch face. "We'll get to them later." She leaned in close to my ear in a way my mother couldn't hear. "Don't try and light any more fires, Moreno. You need training for that, or you'll burn your face off."

Now I knew I didn't like her.

I turned back to my mother. "Wait over there, ok? I'll just be a minute."

I caught up with the colonel and did something I never thought I would do. I stood in front of her and stopped her in her tracks. "Just so you know, I'm not buying it. At least not all of it. I know my file wasn't 'discarded.' I think it's more like someone screwed up, and you haven't figured it out yet. Now, when are you going to give me some real answers?"

I glared at her, but my body held firm in a military rest position. I might be challenging her, but I wasn't about to break rank and get myself written up for insubordination.

For a second, it seemed like that secretive glimmer had returned to her eyes, a sly smile on her lips. "So, someone has been giving you intel." Her face deadpanned.

I actually expected her to reprimand me for speaking out of line, but this time I didn't care. I refused to let my life be the same crapshoot it had been up until now. "Like I said before, we'll talk more later. Now's not the time."

With an icy glare, she motioned for me to move out of the way and kept walking.

Chapter 25

"I. Don't. Know. Anything," I gurgled as Lazear poured water on my face.

I lay flat on a stiff wooden board, blindfolded, my arms and legs strapped down at my sides. My forehead was also restrained so I couldn't twist my head to look at my captor.

Ten seconds had passed since he'd begun torturing me, and although I couldn't see him, I could sense the malicious pleasure he found in this moment. He was savoring it.

"This is simple, Moreno. Just give me the code word, and we can stop. It's entirely up to you." He paused, hovering over me and soaking up this moment.

He placed his hands on either side of the table as I yanked at the straps. I squeezed my lips shut, and he backed away. His footsteps paced somewhere above my head, then he stopped.

"Tell me *now*," he yelled.

I'd been given direct orders not to give up the code word. Repeat the code word, and I failed the mission.

He poured more water over my eyes, nose and mouth. Coughing, I could feel my throat and lungs contract, and we'd only been at it for about fifteen seconds. At this point I'd lost my ability to read his aura. I was struggling. But I held my ground.

"You're just making this worse for yourself," he said, pouring an unreasonable amount of water all over my face, filling my nostrils and smothering my mouth.

I was suffocating. The restraints suddenly felt even tighter. I pulled against them. I wanted to yell but my voice remained confined inside my throat. My head shook back and forth in panic. This was too much.

He stopped pouring. "Now, what's that code word?" he asked calmly. He must've leaned over, for his voice sounded only inches away from my right ear. He was too calm. Almost playful.

I wouldn't cave, but I had to tell him something. "Operation Extra," I choked out.

"Operation Extra, is that right?" Judging by his tone, he seemed to think he had me.

"Yes, that's it." I wriggled my hands, trying to get one loose.

I kept wriggling, but the restraints were too tight. In these months of training, I'd been practicing raising fire to my palms. It was sloppy, but the only way I could figure out how to do it was to focus on my rage. Rage against my father for those nights he'd left me, my mother and my brother terrorized. Rage against my ex for trying to control and manipulate me. And rage against the vampire TI for raising so many primal desires in me for all the wrong reasons.

I harnessed all the rage I could. I channeled it into my hands and focused on my right hand. I brought the fire forward and felt my palms ignite with heat. Yes, I could burn through this strap. My fire would only last a second, but at this close proximity to the strap, it might be all I needed.

I heard Lazear shuffling somewhere behind me. Shit, I'd probably give myself away if I burned through the strap, but I couldn't stop myself. I had to channel my compounded rage.

"I never heard of Operation Extra," he said. "What does that even mean? I think you're making it up."

"Operation Extra"—I coughed—"is a humanitarian operation to bring extra supplies to the refugees here in Colombia. I'm with a nonprofit. I don't know anything. All I do is bring food and clothes to these people."

"Ha, you expect me to believe you? Then why were you carrying weapons?" he asked, probably holding a bucket with more water to douse me if he didn't like my answer.

Of course, it wasn't true. I was buying time.

"You know, there are consequences for lying," he snapped.

I would rather take my last breath than give him the code word.

We hated each other. He knew if I said the real code word, I lost the exercise and he won. I heard more movement and guessed he was probably looking over at the instructor for guidance of what to do next. If he pushed my body to the breaking point, if I needed to be resuscitated, he'd be severely reprimanded.

We each had our own objectives. His was to get the code word while keeping me alive. Mine was to hold out for as long as possible without breaking.

I'd been preparing for this. For two weeks, I'd time myself holding my breath underwater. I was up to one minute. When I wasn't doing that, Baine and I simulated waterboarding each other to build up our resistance. I knew I could last thirty seconds without losing my sense of logic and reason. Baine could last forty. But eventually, we would all weaken. This was a form of torture that was impossible to resist. Everyone broke before a minute.

The training instructors calculated our points for this exercise by how long we lasted. Because we were doomed to fail. That was a given. This interrogation style was infamous for its effectiveness in forcing out information from even the hardest of prisoners.

My SERE training was almost complete with only one month to go, and this resilience training was the hardest part of the entire course. I was the only female and yet the highest performing member of the team.

They'd paired me up with Ivan Lazear because he hated me the most. My instructor had never said that aloud, but I could read it all over his aura. I was convinced he wanted someone who wouldn't have any mercy on me. Someone who resented me to his very core and would take pleasure in seeing me squirm.

Over the past eight months of training, I had expanded well into my abilities, truly beginning to master my gift of reading energy, infiltrating dreams and matching the energy of others. It was becoming second nature and gave me an incredible advantage in every exercise. During our drills in the field, I could sense the energy of the animals we hunted before I saw them. All I had to do was line up my arrow, pull back and land the kill before the animal even detected my presence. Being a city girl, I never expected hunting to come so naturally. This helped Trent and me survive the longest in the wild. We had more protein, fat and animal skins for warmth than any of the other cadets.

When it came to the tactical exercises where we were trapped in overturned Humvees or running hostage simulations, all I had to do was read the energy of the TI managing the exercise, and I could calculate my next move. This kept me one step ahead of the other twenty cadets in our program.

My favorite was Combat Training. I could read my opponent's next move before they even made it, which made it easy for me to duck blows and land unexpected punches. I didn't always use my abilities, though. Like when I wanted to practice getting out of holds, especially when Trent was my opponent. I didn't hate it when he pinned me down.

But the water pouring all over my face, well, that drowned out all my senses. I couldn't read energy. I could barely even think. Whenever Trent and I had practiced on our own, I would black out, so this wasn't a surprise. But I felt out of my element, lost and absolutely confused when I was bound, blindfolded and gagged with water.

The water Lazear held sloshed around in its bucket. From the sound of things, I guessed the bucket was just under his face. Now was the time.

I shot the fire through the strap and felt the nylon burn under my grasp. With my right hand loose, I used all my strength to slam the bucket up.

It splashed all over him and hit him in the head. I wasn't sure exactly what happened next, maybe he fumbled backward, but I didn't think I'd knocked him down. He grunted and cursed as I lifted the blindfold off my eyes. He tried to grab my arm, and I swept my hand around to punch him in the face.

In the seconds it took him to shake off my right hook, he stepped over me. I was trying to unstrap my left hand when he grabbed me, pinning my free hand back down by my side. Standing about six feet tall, 250 pounds and jacked, Lazear was the typical jock who couldn't see past his own ego. He had jet-black hair, a defined jaw and golden-hazel eyes I was sure made all the girls on base swoon.

As he held me down, he slapped me across my face with the back of his other hand. It was totally allowed in this type of training exercise, and I made a mental note to slap him around a few times if I ever got out of this.

I gave him a fiery look before I spat at him. He barely blinked. He enjoyed this. He was practically glowing as he removed his belt to replace the ruined strap. He'd probably gained back points for resourcefulness.

"Now, now. We can't have you misbehaving like that, Moreno," he said through gritted teeth. "And I'm going to need to know how you managed to get a fire going in here." He patted down my arm, looking for a lighter.

I could sense he wanted to yell, but he knew that would show the others he was losing his cool. But really, whatever points I lost on this exercise meant absolutely nothing in the overall training program. I was so far ahead I would still be the honor graduate. However, I wouldn't lose a single point to him without a fight.

He placed the blindfold back over my eyes, and I half expected the TI to call my loss. But the instructor let us carry on.

More water poured over my mouth and eyes, and I wasn't ready. My mouth was slightly open, and I forgot to blow the air out of my nose. Water gushed into every crevice as my body jerked and wriggled. My face burn red with pressure as blood rushed to my head. A harsh pounding throbbed along my temples. My throat tightened, my lungs convulsed and my entire body shook uncontrollably. Lazear finally stopped pouring, and for the first time since basic training, I lost count of how long something took.

"Now, Moreno, this is your final chance to tell me," he said. "What is the code word?"

The last thing I remembered was barely choking out the words, "The code word is... *me cago en tu mai, hijo de puta.*"

That's when the last gush of water poured over me, and then I could no longer feel my body. Instead, I felt myself lifting, floating right above the board I was lying on.

In the distance, I barely heard someone yell, *"Stop.* Stop the exercise. No more."

I looked down and saw my body just lying beneath me, not moving as Lazear pressed two fingers into my neck for a pulse. He was still so calm. The TI ran in, and Lazear shook his head.

He just lost the exercise, I thought, satisfied.

And then everything went black.

Chapter 26

In the dark, off in the distance, there was a familiar spark of the same deep purple color that made up my aura. I moved toward it, not sure if I was walking or floating. The only thought in my mind was to get to that glowing purple, star-like shape on the distant horizon. But the closer I moved, the farther away it slipped.

But where was I? I looked around. I must have passed out. I couldn't see my legs, arms or body. I was just a floating thing.

I must be able to move faster like this, without the weight of a physical form.

I willed it and closed in on the deep purple light. As I got closer, I noticed the all-too-familiar deep, ominous Shadow surrounding the light. The light would've been brighter if it hadn't been for all the mist and fury blocking what was beyond it. After all I'd been through, I was no longer scared of the Shadow.

I sped closer to the opening and wove my energy into the dark canvas surrounding me. I could finally see through the hole in between the shadows where the light was coming from.

There I was, standing inside the swirling, black monster cloud with its blighted souls twisting around in its center. They tried to pull me along with them as they always did. Tempting me with promises of passion, drawing me in with lust and desires that only the dark could satisfy. Alluring as it was, I had lots of practice resisting them by now so I could concentrate on what was happening in the center.

A woman's back was to me. She was dressed all in black and had her long black hair up in a tight ponytail. It was twilight, and she was in a woody area with a barn behind her. In an instant, the night rippled around her in a mist of black as her hands touched the ground, and the rest of her body transformed into slivers of shadow.

Where her human form had been, appeared a massive black jaguar, twice the size of any jaguar I had ever seen. The beast broke into a run so fast and furious I almost lost her. I willed myself behind her, flying in the air above and following the creature quickly into a cave aglow with embers. The crimson glow from the embers trailed up the walls, where dozens of carved symbols pulsed faintly with the light. They pulsed in rhythm. Glowing and softening, as though they were the living, beating heart of the cave I was entering.

Some of the shapes were familiar, like the Taino sun and spirals I'd seen in books. But others I couldn't name – beasts or spirits too ancient for me to recognize.

The symbols pulsed like they knew me. Being in this state of shadows and mist, I could sense a strong sort of knowing that I was exactly where I needed to be. Like this cave, these symbols and the ancestors from this place, had been waiting for me to come back. A piece of me — something buried and wild — stirred awake.

The shadows rippled once again into a mist-covered human form crouched on the ground. As the feral body stood, I recognized her.

She was me.

Standing naked, her toned arms, legs and abdomen projected the kind of power and savage confidence of an animal, not a human. Her shining, long black hair, now loose, fell over her tan shoulders and gently framed her breasts. As she turned around to look at me, her eyes commanded me in with the same now-familiar dark energy.

I hesitated only because I didn't like being forced into anything. But with a slight tilt of her head, it became impossible to resist the pull of her deep, rich-green eyes. I could feel her energy already coursing through me, filling me with such delicious power. She nodded slightly, as if acknowledging my apprehension, understanding it.

It was then that I let go and trusted.

It took all the resilience from my mental agility training to keep me from jumping right back out of her. The energy surging through this creature was super-charged and spiking bolts of energy straight into my center of consciousness. At first I had nothing to grab on to, nothing to center me as everything around me became a jumbled-up haze. She could do whatever she wanted.

Noticing my panic, she gently pulled back on the energy surge. "Sasha, you have got to wake up soon," her voice echoed inside my mind. "But before you do, you must remember what I am about to tell you. The power running through you doesn't come from the Zodiac. It comes from your ancestors, here on your island. This has always been your fate. Before the Houses. Before time itself. But you must find your shaman. He is in the market, hiding. He doesn't want to come back. But don't give up. You must convince him, otherwise you'll never cross the Gate in time." She knelt at the edge of the fire burning inside the cave. "Forget the world you thought you knew, it doesn't exist. The Houses are always testing you."

Now that my eyes were her eyes, I peered through them as she stared into the fire. The flames shifted, and a battle unfolded within them. Military forces fought a ground war against epic beasts. Bloodied and fanged dragons, wolves, fae, and vampires ripped apart humans. The human weapons were useless, powerless.

In between the crimson flickers of light, I couldn't understand why tanks, cars and fighter planes were all stagnant. Not moving. There was no energy, no light, no power in sight.

The scene shot a fierce chill straight through me, and I felt a rising panic as I realized the familiar world—my world—was ravaged. The Sasha-form I possessed lifted a hand, pointing to the fringes of the battle. The beast she had become moments ago stood on the edge, watching the fight with blood dripping from too-sharp canines. At that moment, I tasted metallic blood in my own mouth.

I watched that magnificent version of myself lift her hand to her mouth and touch her lips. When she was done, I looked at her fingers. They were stained with blood.

"First blood," was the last thing I heard before my mind faded to black once again.

My head felt heavy as I turned it to the left. I slowly opened my eyes, and everything was blurry. I could only make out a few things, like a square window, the neatly made bed I was in with yellow sheets and a small table to my right.

I closed my eyes again and wiggled my fingers and toes. It felt good to be back in my own skin, but I was tired. My sore wrists, legs, neck and arms felt as heavy as lead when I tried to move them. Wherever I was felt safe for now. I drifted off again.

Sometime later, I opened my eyes to the sound of the door opening. It was Trent.

"Hey," he said. He pushed a button on the wall, and a nurse came in. They took my vitals and asked me how I was feeling. When they left, Trent stayed behind.

"You feeling ok?" he asked.

"Yeah, just sore. And tired."

"You had us all worried." He took a seat in the chair next to my bed. He came into focus as I sought out those familiar, deep-blue eyes of his. Golden stubble lined his jaw, and despite his cool façade, I could tell he was more than a little concerned.

Chapter 27

"What do you mean? What happened?" I asked, realizing I was in the medic hut.

There were no hospitals in our makeshift training center in Cartagena, Colombia. All we had was one doctor, one nurse and the basic equipment to keep us performing at our highest levels. This included regular vitamin infusions, immunizations, vaccinations, cryotherapy and occasional steroid injections for muscle recovery after injuries.

"You died," he said.

"I what?"

My eyes wanted to open wide, but couldn't. I moved to sit up, but he gently put his hand on my shoulder and eased me back down.

"You need to rest, ok? Your heart completely stopped for ten minutes or more. We aren't sure exactly how long. But you were gone, Sasha. I thought I'd lost you."

My heart became heavy as I looked in his familiar blue eyes. His chest oozed gray and indigo energy; pain from the loss of his mother less than a year ago was still fresh there. This wasn't good for him.

"It's going to take a lot more than death to keep me away," I joked.

"Ha," he scoffed, smiling warmly.

He reached for my hand and squeezed it gently. I squeezed back and pulled him to me. My vision wasn't so blurry anymore. I took in his broad shoulders and sun-rinsed features.

He hovered over me and leaned down to plant a gentle kiss on my forehead. Before he could pull away, I reached my hand up and touched my lips. He moved his head lower to press his lips against mine. And the warm sensation that arose within me reminded me why I enjoyed being alive.

I remembered our first kiss. We were on a training exercise in a forest in Montana before we'd been cleared to go to Colombia. We broke off in pairs, and since I was the only girl in our group, I got to pick who I paired off with. Of course I chose Trent.

We had to use the skills we'd learned living off the land, and at least with me, he knew he would have plenty of protein in his diet. We found a place to camp by a lake and had just finished off a rabbit soup complete with wild roots, berries and herbs. Lying on our sleeping bags, we talked under the bright, swollen moon.

He told me a crazy story about his friends back home, how one time they went camping by a lake like this one and the only food they'd brought were burgers. They didn't even bring buns or condiments, just the meat, and that was all they ate for three days.

I was laughing when he looked over at me, his eyes glistening in the moonlight. His chest, rising and falling with his breaths, called my hands to run over the bare skin just underneath his T-shirt.

He must've noticed how I bit my bottom lip and stared into his deep blue eyes, because he leaned over and pressed his firm lips to mine. His tongue slid across my teeth and connected with my mouth in a way that sent warmth coursing through my body.

He placed one hand on my side and the other on my neck, and every inch of my body tingled at his caress. He slid his hands to my waist and held me there. I touched him back, feeling the contours of his abs under my hands, firm and unyielding. His growing erection pressed against my thigh.

He slid his fingers into my center and stroked me until I let out a soft, wanting moan. When I did, he covered my mouth with another kiss, this one more passionate than the last.

"I've wanted to do that for months," he whispered.

I smiled. "Me, too."

He told me that night he never thought he could feel so much for a person. After he'd lost his mom, he didn't think his heart could take losing someone he loved again.

We were both hurting and found healing in each other's embrace. My mind wasn't ready to admit that I loved him, but my heart already screamed it.

"Those lips are worth coming back from the dead for," I said with a soft smile.

He returned my smile and sat back down in the chair next to my hospital bed. "Oh, check this out." He reached into his pocket to pull out his phone. "Your horoscope for today said, 'You have recently closed a chapter of your life, and today offers you the chance to make a fresh start of things. Use the lessons of your past to build a better future. Seek the help of others, especially those who can show you the way.'"

"Sounds about right," I said softly.

"So, what was it like, when you went out?"

"It was all black. I don't remember anything," I told him. I couldn't tell him what I saw; he wouldn't understand. I still didn't even understand. It meant something, but what? "Hey, can you get me a notebook and something to write with?"

"Um, sure. Yeah, give me a second." He got up and left the room.

I stared out the window at the rolling hills and rooftops. I imagined the air outside must be crisp with the sun shining bright through the clouds.

Trent returned and handed me the notebook. I set it down on the table next to me to write in later. Although my body felt sore all over, I was filled with a delicious sense of pride that I'd never given in to Lazear and an even deeper satisfaction that he'd get reprimanded for it.

"What happened to Lazear?" I asked, hoping he'd at least lost points because of my death.

I couldn't remember how many times the TIs had told us we couldn't let our hostages die. That the hostage was more valuable alive than dead. If we allowed the hostage to die, we failed the mission.

A fire rose in my chest as I remembered him pinning me down after I'd punched him. The look on his face.

"Sasha, really? You're asking about Lazear?" Trent gaped at me. "You *died*." He shook his head in disbelief. "Let's just be glad you came back. But just so you know, he's recovering from a broken nose right now." He grinned and rubbed the knuckles of his right hand.

I soaked that in for a moment. The thought of my life almost having been lost washed over me with ripples across my skin.

He softened a bit while searching my eyes, and I wanted to drown in his. "What was that even like?" Trent asked. "Did you have any visions?"

"It was..." I stopped as the memories came flooding back. It was all so familiar, yet so strange. I closed my eyes, seeing the deep purple light in the distance, trying to remember the words that had echoed in my mind, the words that were my own.

"It was what?" he asked sincerely. No hidden agenda lay behind his eyes that matched the clear sky outside.

"I can't remember. I need to sleep now." I gently closed my eyes.

The next day I was released, cleared to go back to duty after three days off for recovery. Miguel Perez, our commanding officer (CO), asked me lots of questions about the fire, but I just denied any knowledge of it. I mean, they couldn't prove it, and to claim I had fire powers would get me sent to psych evals instantly.

When I found out Lazear had received fifteen days of extra duty and thirty days of restriction, it bothered me that that wasn't nearly the maximum punishment for actually killing someone. But I felt better knowing at least Trent had gotten a punch in.

I appreciated the time off. I hadn't had this many days off in months. I finally had time alone and wondered a lot about what it meant to be a nagual. The gifts of reading auras, of seeing the energy of life, was not lost on me. Neither was my ability to run faster, withstand the elements better and outperform any woman I had ever met. It was unheard of, especially of a woman with my lean stature, yet here I was.

I wondered about the Joint Zodiac Command, the Houses of the Zodiac, and I wanted to learn what had happened to that shitbag vampire Grange. More than that, I was growing anxious because I wasn't any closer to finding the shaman. And Colonel van Holst wasn't taking any of my requests for a meeting. I hadn't heard from her since we'd spoken months ago at my graduation. All she said was I would be stationed in Colombia, and the shaman was believed to be there.

Chapter 28

My vision told me I would find the shaman in the market, so I decided to start searching there. As I strolled through the alleyways lined with stalls of fresh fruit, vegetables and local food, the cool air was filled with the whispers. I'd dressed as a civilian with black jeans, a loose white tank top and black Converse, my hair left down and blown out.

Now, just a day after my death, an energy surged through me that heightened my senses even more. My fingertips prickled with an unusual heat. A metallic taste filled my mouth, and I could hear the whispers in the wind carried down from the clouds. An ancient wind, I could faintly hear words of an unfamiliar language spoken when it swept by my hair. It wasn't the piercing screeching of the Zodiac Shadows. No, this was something else.

I was picking up frozen arepas when a blast of the whispery wind thrummed around me. I bent over to retrieve a green pepper that'd fallen on the floor, and when I straightened, the shop was full of artesanias. Funny, I didn't see them here a minute ago.

Colorful woven baskets, purses and leather jewelry lined the shop perfumed with rich earth and sandalwood. I was drawn into the space, everything about it called to me, the warm smell filling my lungs.

A young woman about my age sat at the counter reading manga. Her hair was thick, straight and dark, with light curls at the ends. Her makeup was done perfectly, and her aura glowed a bright yellow.

Everything in this store called out to me. The baskets were colorful and so intricately woven the idea of them brought me to another time, another world. There were fine purses and belts, and when I checked the price tags on some of the items, I clearly couldn't afford any of it.

As I was about to leave, the whispers grew louder, but I couldn't make out the words. I felt a tugging in my center, pulling me near a presence. An energy just like mine. This was the first time since I'd accepted my abilities that this had happened.

I looked around the shop for signs of the dark energy or an aura with a glow like mine. Anything to explain the sounds and smells wafting around me. I walked farther into the cluttered shop, turning myself sideways between clothing racks and basket displays. The back of the store was stocked floor to ceiling with even more baskets. But there, covered by a thin white curtain, was a small opening. I couldn't see any hint of shadow or colorful energy back there. But the sounds were louder. I slowly pulled the curtain back a few inches and stole a look inside.

I flinched when I discovered a man standing at the entrance, staring directly at me. He was much taller than me, with intense emerald eyes and a rough, short black beard. Our eyes met, and an electric shock tingled through my body. I was drawn to him. My soul felt like I'd seen him countless times before, but my eyes told me I had not.

Was this the Shaman? It had to be.

His shoulders were broad, and he definitely looked like he worked out. He didn't look like the mystical Shaman I fancied up in my imagination. I pictured an old guy with a long beard, not a rugged-but-sexy guy in his late twenties. My shoulders tensed at the sight of him. Under normal circumstances I would've been lured in by his strikingly gorgeous features, but something about his posture and the way he glared at me made me uneasy. His thick black eyebrows were two perfect lines that hardened his already sharp features. He was at once both striking and commanding.

"You." He clicked his tongue and lifted his chin, unimpressed.

"What?" I scoffed, feeling like a scolded eight-year-old.

I straightened; my military training made me apprehensive of this whole situation. I should've turned around and walked out, now. For the first time since this had all started, I couldn't read a person's energy. But that wouldn't stop me. I could handle myself now. I wasn't the same insecure girl I'd been when I'd joined the military. Lost in my own mind. Afraid. Broken. I needed to find the Shaman, and I had to know if this was him.

"Come in, you miserable creature. Let's get this over with." He practically spat the words with distaste.

"Um, I don't even know you." How could he hate me without even knowing me?

"I have known you for centuries," he growled.

Turning away, he disappeared deeper into the store. From his walk and the way he was dressed, he came across as robust and refined, like finely aged whisky. Yet his words were more like the cheaper well drinks.

"Ale, don't come back here for a while," he told the girl at the counter.

I didn't want to follow him, but something pulled me after him. The white curtain hid a dimly lit hallway, and I scanned every corner for the deep ripples of shadow that lined everything, good or bad. Nothing.

At the end of the hall, he entered a small room rich with the scent of sandalwood. I stopped at the door. This could be a trap. A breeze brushed my skin, and the whispers nudged me forward.

Chapter 29

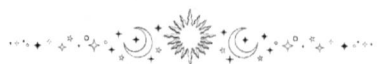

I wouldn't step into the room.

He stood in front of an altar lined with three rows of colored candles with images painted on them. Crystals and small wooden carvings of animals, Jesus, Mary and the saints clustered around the candles. He began to arrange them, picking them up and moving them about with no apparent pattern.

I watched his hands carefully. With shoulders hunched over, he turned his head slightly and peeked at me from the corner of his eye, mumbling words to himself. Why couldn't I read his energy?

"Estrellas, los santos, que hace aquí esta… maldición?" he mumbled.

Was he talking about me? Now this guy was starting to piss me off. "I am not a curse."

I wasn't going to stand there and take insults for no reason. I made to leave when his hand reached into the candles and pulled out a gun. Faster than I could blink, he held the gun with both hands and pointed it directly at my head.

"Are you sure about that?"

The question vibrated through me. My eyes flicked between his face and the gun. He was dead serious. I should've known he was crazy.

"I am not sending you to the Gates if that's what you came here for," he said, holding the gun steady at my head. "So, you can just leave."

So, he *was* the Shaman.

My heart threatened to beat out of my chest as a blaze of heat ignited. I wasn't about to die twice in two days. What kind of shitty week was I having?

The heat in my chest and at the tips of my fingers blazed even hotter, so hot they felt like they were literally on fire. I was so afraid he was going to shoot me, but I had to look at my hands because the heat was way too intense.

When I lifted them, a bolt of fire coursed out of the tips of my fingers and shot directly toward him.

The fire pressed him against the back wall. He lifted both arms to protect his face, gun still in hand. When the flames dissipated, he stole a look over his arms.

I knew I couldn't truly call on the fire whenever I wanted to, but he didn't.

"Put the gun down, or I'll do it again." I hoped he wouldn't call my bluff.

"Fine." He grimly set the gun on a small table in the room.

I snatched it up, removed the magazine and cleared the chamber. I slid the bullets into my pocket and placed the empty nine-millimeter back down on the table.

"Seems the stars favor you." His face was dark and anything but welcoming. "At least the fire signs do." I was momentarily distracted by his elegant accent.

"Look, I don't know a whole lot about all this, but what I do know is you've been MIA for way too long. I need to cross the Gate, and my time is running out."

The rage inside me was growing again. I could feel the fire rising from within, and a strange shift of energy swirled inside me. I inhaled deeply.

"No, you can't." He shook his head and took a seat in a large leather chair behind a beautifully carved wooden desk.

Without a gun trained on my forehead, I was finally able to take in the breadth of the room. Polished terra-cotta tiles, white leather furniture and eclectic vases and relics had been placed sparingly throughout. It felt both modern and rich with culture all at once.

I shut the door behind me. Right now, I had to keep my cool and gather intel. I took another look at my fingers, expecting the tips to be burned off. They were only slightly red, and normal sensations were returning. When I returned my attention to the shaman, he'd softened a little.

"Sit down, have a drink with me." It sounded like more like an order than a question.

I almost sat, but then it dawned on me this complete stranger had an unhealthy amount of pull in my life. If I didn't comply, he wouldn't help me. If he didn't help me, I'd go crazy. There was no way I could let anyone have that kind of power over me. Yet here I was, hanging on his every word.

"No, thanks." I forced out.

"Well, I will." He poured himself a russet-colored drink from one of those fancy crystal containers. "You need my help, you know."

"Ok, yes. On second thought, pour me a drink, too."

A drink would go a long way right now. Especially a drink that smooth and rich. The frown on his smoldering face lessened as he handed me a glass. I made sure to sip it slowly, allowing the vibrant flavors to fill my alcohol-deprived tastebuds for a few fleeting seconds.

I wasn't sure how to make this guy help me, especially if I couldn't read or adjust his energy. But I wouldn't give up. I didn't want to go crazy. *You must convince him, otherwise you won't cross the Gate in time.*

"The Celestial Decree has bound me to you and you to me." He swirled the liquid in his glass and returned to his chair.

Confused, I sat in the chair across from him, still searching for an aura I couldn't see.

He leaned back and casually crossed his legs.

Chapter 30

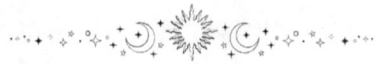

"Yes, I am your shaman, and I know exactly who you are," he said, completely void of emotion, feeling and energy.

But wait, what was that in his eyes? Was that intrigue or something else?

"Let me be the first to congratulate you in getting this far," he droned. You have grown up to be quite a beautiful lady."

"Thanks, I guess. Does that mean you knew me when I was younger?"

"Yes, Sasha. I watched you from the shadows when you were a child. I never thought you would make it this far without me. I was hoping you wouldn't."

I wanted to throw my drink in his face.

"Ok, first of all, you're an asshole. Why not?" Somehow, I was not at all surprised.

He sat up in his chair and leaned toward me, eyes laser-sharp and focused. "You might not think so, but you are a curse. All of you nagual are."

"Ok. Sounds like some personal shit to me. Can't you tell the Zodiac Command to assign me to someone else? Why do I have to suffer because of whatever crawled up your ass and died?" I asked, trying to keep my voice from shaking.

A flash of green flared from the top of his head. His aura.

I stared deep into his emerald eyes flecked with shards of jade. Without thinking, I pulled the green energy I saw tucked away in those shards toward me. If I couldn't read his energy, I would read his soul.

It was trapped in those shards of his eyes, and I released him from his confinement. I matched my energy to the white of his shirt, the white of the tiny flecks in his energy centers and covered him with the purity of the crown chakra.

As I held his energy—or was it his soul?—suspended in the air, I realized I was giving him freedom from himself. Freedom from the belief that I was not worth his trouble. I separated this and every other sharp, broken and shattered thought that created his dark energy.

I broke his energy into the tiniest of pieces to be scattered away with the shadows of the wind. A pure energy source remained, floating freely in the space between us.

This energy was fluid in the air—a liquid, a gas and a mist all at once. Light and free, I watched it hover over his body below. This floating essence went rigid and bolted upward. It slammed into a black shadow wall that I'd created, and it couldn't escape. I used the force of the darkness to shove his unwilling energy back into his body.

The shaman blinked slowly, sitting up in his chair. "Well, this time you came bearing gifts." His voice was calm and centered, a white aura surrounding him.

That was such a cool trick; I kind of hoped he'd be a dick again so I could keep practicing. But what did he mean by "this time?" I had never seen him before.

"You know, I'm not the one you're sick of," I said. "You're sick of yourself, being alive for so long. Bored of the role you've had for so many years. I get it, I really do. But it's not my fault. I refuse to go down just because you can't handle your boring immortal life and the job of preparing us naguals for our training." I felt a squirming underneath my chest, a flash of energy shooting through me.

Even after what I'd said, his shoulders were still relaxed, not all tense and aggravated as he studied me. "I know you feel her, your jaguar. She's ready to be released."

"No shit. And the second she's released, she's coming for you."

He chuckled, but I wasn't joking.

"How did you learn that... that trick with the energy? That's very useful. And it's new. I like new things. It's true I'm tired of this routine." Two bolts of dark energy shot through his white aura, the familiar Shadow creeping back in. He cocked his head to one side. "Can you do it again?"

"Of course I can. And I could burn this entire place down if I wanted to."

Sure, I was bluffing, but he was considering my offer. Perhaps considering that I wasn't his enemy.

"Well, that's impressive." He smiled widely. "I hid my energy from you so you couldn't find me. Seems all I did was delay the inevitable."

"Why don't you start by telling me why I couldn't read your aura before?" I asked.

"Oh, ha. I retracted it. But the second you found me, my wards could no longer work on you because of our bond. I must admit, I'm more than a little impressed. You'll get lots of extra points at the Academy for finding me with my energy retracted.

"You also broke through all of my wards by finding this place without me knowing. I still don't know how you did that. And I'm sure you'll get even more points for controlling your mind, finding your elemental power and whatever that little trick was you did with my energy. That felt... surreal. It was pretty badass."

He'd sounded pleased, but then his expression turned dark, and he retracted his aura again. What was with this guy? Nothing was easy.

"Thanks. I guess. I mean, if it was up to you, I'd be locked up in a psych ward. Mind finally explaining to me what Zol Stria actually is, and what are the Gates?" I asked. "Think of the rings of a tree trunk. The tree exists, complete with all its rings. But there are inner rings and outer rings, right? The outermost ring is the one you're looking at, and the inner rings are hidden inside. Earth is the outer ring. It's the version of the world you can see as a human, and it works as an entry point into all of the other rings. And the inner rings are Zol Stria. There are exactly twelve rings within Zol Stria, one for each Zodiac House." He took another sip of whisky.

I inched forward, ready to ask another question when he began again.

"The Joint Celestial Command is where Earth's military intelligence works together with Zol Stria's Gatekeepers," he continued. "Zol Stria agrees not to pillage the Earth and vice versa. Now, humans are at a disadvantage, because the creatures of Zol Stria are far more powerful than any human, and they can be vicious and bloodthirsty. That's where you and I come in. We're humans with the ability to travel to Zol Stria and back. The stars designed us to work in teams to keep balance and protect the veil."

He got up to pour himself another drink, and I got a chance to notice how snug his pants fit him from behind. He may be centuries old, but he definitely didn't look like it.

"So, what is there to protect?" I asked.

When he finished pouring, he replaced the cap and sat back down. "Well, there has got to be order on both sides. If we just let anyone cross the veil, on either side of the Gates, there are vulnerabilities. The demons, vampires and basilisks would feast on human flesh. Earth is the only entry point between the twelve Gates, so the Zodiac Houses formed a decree to allow humanity to thrive so they could cross the Gates in a neutral environment where none of the Houses truly dominate.

"In a power-thirsty star system, this is how we ensure no one House has too much power. Our kind, shaman and nagual, are the designated liaisons between our dimensions. Your role, when you graduate, will be to take down the veil jumpers that break the accord."

I stared blankly at him as confusion dripped through me like wax from a candle. "Ok, so the only way to go between the Gates is on Earth?"

"Yes."

"So, it's not like the rings of a tree, but instead it's just like the zodiac wheel, where Earth is the big circle in the middle of all the signs of the zodiac?"

"Precisely."

My analogy was so much better than his about the tree rings, but his expression gave away nothing.

I wanted to laugh. "So, you are saying humans know about the Gates?"

"Well, they did hundreds of years ago until they were glamoured. Only the human members of the Command know about it now, and the half-humans among our populations."

"Oh, of course. The Command, makes sense," I scoffed and sat back in my chair.

I scanned the room to see if this whole thing was being recorded by Lazear and his crew as some kind of elaborate scheme to prove me psychologically unfit to finish SERE training. "I do have more questions."

I wanted to believe there was more to my unique "condition" that made sense, even if it sounded absurd. Plus, I couldn't just skim over the fact that future-Sasha had told me to listen to this asshole.

"Of course you do," he said. "We'll make an exchange. A question for a question. But let's get out of here. I could use some fresh air."

We walked out the same way I'd come in, and as I opened the front door of the shop, I noticed all the merchandise was gone. Not only in front of his shop, but all the shops in the alley were gone. The bustling market I'd seen just a few minutes ago had disappeared, and there was only a street lined with buildings.

When I looked over at the shaman, the corner of his lips lifted into a smirk.

Chapter 31

"Wait, what happened to the market?"

He walked ahead, not acknowledging me. Seriously, what was up with this guy?

I met his pace, and we walked in silence for a few blocks until we reached a corner restaurant with small tables and chairs outside. I was drawn to him, as though an invisible string tethered us together. This all felt like it had happened before. We were on an overlook to a river below, and the curve of the river and the position of the café seemed entirely too familiar. I stared into the water. I wasn't sure what I was looking for, but I didn't find it.

"Here, sit here." He motioned to a chair and walked inside.

I sat, and he returned with two glasses and a bottle of whisky. He poured our drinks, and I watched his biceps tighten under his shirt. When he was finished, I switched our glasses.

"Drink first." I pushed his glass toward him.

He broke his solemn expression with a laugh and took a sip. When nothing happened, I took a sip of mine.

"You put me in a good mood, Nagual. This doesn't happen often. We may be off to a better start than the last time you came around. At least, I hope so."

"Well, that sounds promising," I said sarcastically. "And when was that, the last time I came around? Even though I can't recall ever being here before."

"The Zodiac Houses rule over Zol Stria, and since you are the nagual reborn, you are an asset to them."

My face deadpanned. What the what?

"Ok, so I know Lily taught you about the different zodiac systems of the world. Well, the Zodiac Houses oversee them all and they operate under a master zodiac calendar. The master calendar dictated when you, Sasha Moreno, would be born. Just like it dictates the birth of all nagual. You carry in your DNA the genes of all the nagual who have come before you. You, in particular, were reborn 225 years after the last nagual with whom you share DNA, making you a nagual reborn.

"The Zodiac Houses are guided by the principles that every single human being is a miniature version of the cosmos, and everything in nature has a parallel in human beings. Therefore, the universe is linked to all humankind through a system of correlations."

Good thing I had the whisky in my hand. I took another sip to ease down the information he was giving me.

"Now I get to ask a question," he said. "How did you learn that trick, with my energy?"

"I got the idea from a vision I had. The vision came to me when I died."

None of what I'd just said had any effect on him. He didn't even flinch. Normal humans didn't act like that.

"Oh, so you've already had a Progression. Without my help. The stars favor you indeed."

Judging by the tilt of his head and the way his mouth curled, he seemed at least a little impressed.

"My turn," I said. "What happens when I complete the training?"

"You become a Master Nagual and work for the Zodiac Arcane Forces, the defenders of Zol Stria." He leaned back in his chair. "I have guided twenty nagual, and not all of them have become Masters. That fire you shot at me is fueled by the control you've taken of your own darkness. You still aren't pulling in the darkness in from around you. That's why you only have one quick blast at a time. I know you don't have any more than that." He chuckled to himself and sat back.

Ok, so bluff called.

"You'll get to that," he assured. "But I'm surprised you've even gotten as far as controlling your mind on your own. I only remember one other nagual doing that without training, a few centuries back."

In the corner of my eye, I picked up on the darkness swirling around us. It was as if at the mere mention of the dark shadowy mist that seemed an endless abyss, it would come to the forefront.

"Now once you learn how to harness all of this"—he gestured to the dark clouds I thought only I could see—"well, I'm sure you can imagine what you might be capable of. It's my turn now. Who did that to your neck?"

At the mention of my neck, it started to throb.

"Oh." I reached up and rubbed it. "I don't know. What do you mean? Do you see something?"

"Yes, there's a concentration of spell-laced venom there. A vampire has claimed you as theirs," he said gravely.

"That was from the TI in basic training. Don't worry, I had him arrested."

He laughed so heartily he clutched his sides. "Ok, sure. He was arrested." He chuckled some more. "Now it's your turn."

"What are you laughing at?" My eyes bulged. "You don't think he's been arrested?"

"Maybe he was at first, but I'm sure that didn't last long. He's not a threat to Zol Stria, or I'd know about him. And if he's not a threat to Zol Stria, he's pretty much free to do what he wants."

I gaped at him for the briefest heartbeat.

"Help me understand something, if he's a vampire, how is it he can be out in broad daylight? I thought they couldn't be exposed to UV rays or something."

Damian replied, "Vampires can be in the sun during the weeks of their sun sign. And whenever it's not, they just need to raise a deflector spell. You'll learn how to do that, too. It's a sort of magical shield that protects you from things your magic is otherwise vulnerable to." I nodded, somehow trying to understand all this.

"Well in that case, what if I don't want to become a Gatekeeper? I mean, this whole system seems stupid anyway. I don't want to go 'mad' like they told me I would, but I don't think I will. I've come this far on my own. What do I need the Academy for?"

I had purpose now. I finally belonged somewhere. I was falling for Trent in a big way. He accepted me for who I was. He never made me feel bad about myself, and he was there for me when I needed him. I never knew what it was to be accepted until now, with him. I wasn't ready to let him go and run off to some supernatural training in a world full of monsters.

"That's entirely true," he said, swirling his whisky. "You have done well on your own, so far. Take your chances. Don't join the Academy. Go back to your boyfriend and the human world you're comfortable with."

"It'd be a shame to waste your gifts. I'm only sitting here, after dodging this role for this long, because of what you did with my dark energy back there in my shop. I'm impressed, to say the least, and there's more to all of this than you can even imagine."

I remembered the vision I'd had on my hospital bed. The fighting, the blood and the destruction.

"Now that you've found me, the wards I had in place to keep my location hidden have weakened. I'm obliged by our bond to help you." He sighed unhappily. "It is my curse."

Chapter 32

"You haven't shifted into your jaguar yet. And when you do, when that beast comes out of you, let's just say you haven't even seen crazy yet. Without training, she will rip into any human in your path." The shaman's eyes became hooded, and his face darkened even more. "Children, babies, lovers, she won't care. All she wants is her First Blood. And there's one more thing. There's a shortage of nagual. I don't know why, but every Transit there are fewer and fewer in the program."

The vision of blood dripping from my lips and the taste in my mouth made me salivate. I tried to control the trembling in my bones as an icy current shot through them. "When will I shift?"

"At the close of your Transit of the Twelfth House, which is just next week." He seemed worried for me then, as if he still had a trickle of humanity left.

"That's why the dreams said I would go mad by then."

"Yes, because if the darkness hasn't made you mad already, your jaguar definitely will. The first step is to control your thoughts. Congratulations, you managed to do that." He lifted his cup in a mock salute. "This means the stars have granted you the next stage in your evolution, which is shifting. However, when you shift, the jaguar will take over. You must shift within Zol Stria to be able to shift back into your human form. That is the only place where I can cast my spells of celestial transformation."

He was talking about the black jaguar I shifted into in my dreams and visions. The energy I saw clearly that no one else did. The fire in my hands. My enhanced senses, speed and abilities at field-training exercises. The pieces were beginning to come together.

"Ok, well I don't even know your name, and you've been hiding for so long, how can I believe you?" I knew I had to trust him because of what future-Sasha had told me, but I wanted to hear it from him.

"My apologies."

"I'm Damian, and I don't care if you believe me. For all these years, I've been searching for a way to break my bond to the nagual, and I haven't found it. I'm still working on it, though. If you walk away, which you are welcome to do, I won't chase after you. I'd rather chain myself to a wall."

He leaned back in his chair and took a drink, resolute. It seemed he had given this some thought.

I stood up, ready to walk away, and that's when he whispered a few words in an unfamiliar, guttural language and set a long, pointed crystal of rose quartz on the table.

"Here, take this with you," he said.

"What is it?"

"This is your training crystal. It will help you channel all the shadow energy. With this, you will see the world as I see the world. As it really is."

"What do you mean, *as it really is*?" I sat back down, lifting the glass of whisky to my lips and swallowing the rest in one burning gulp.

"You want the world to be one way, so that is what you see. It is what you are taught and what your parents were taught. It is the glamour all humans have over their eyes. Now if you channel the shadows that surround you into this crystal, you will get glimpses of the world that is hidden from you, until you no longer need the crystal."

"So, it shows the truth?"

"Well, I wouldn't go that far. It shows you the unseen, the world of magic and stars, that you aren't capable of seeing because of your limited human vision. But as a nagual who's not gone mad, you are able to see much more of the unseen than others. With this stone, you can use your abilities to access the entire scope of the unseen world before you become a Master. But it isn't a truth stone. In both Zol Stria and here, there will always be secrets."

My mind went to Trent. The more I spoke to Damian, the further I was from ever having a normal life with him.

"Still don't believe me?" he asked. "Let's try it. Hold the crystal in your right hand and tell me what you feel."

As soon as I picked it up, the prickly charge warmed my palm. "It has energy." I flicked my gaze to meet his.

"Yes, now all you have to do is channel all those Shadows through there and direct them toward the area you want exposed."

I almost laughed. "Wait, you see my Shadows?"

"They aren't your shadows. They're just energy. And yes, I see everything you see, and a whole lot more."

"But wait, there are creatures in the dark mist that I see. One of them burned my knee and left a scar. How is that energy?"

"Those beasts are your path," he answered. "For an eternity, you have hunted their kind and entrapped them. Why wouldn't their kind try to keep you from becoming who you truly are? From becoming powerful enough to stop them?"

"And how am I supposed to send these shadows through the crystal?"

"How have you done any of the things you do?" he answered my question with a question as only a teacher could.

As much as I wanted to get up and walk away from all of this, a deeper part of me was compelled to listen. It was the part of me that had so many questions I needed to understand.

I held the crystal in my hand and closed my eyes. I perpetually sensed the Shadows. They were always there, lurking in the dark corners and whispering their dark words. I imagined them coming together, intertwining and folding over themselves into a funnel. When I opened my eyes, several shadow tornados had materialized around me.

"You need my spells, Nagual. That is why I am here. To teach you. You've done well herding your shadows, now you must say the words *I'ic il taak* while holding the crystal."

"Wait, what? What language is that?"

"It's a combination. All of my spells use a combination of words from the ancient languages of this land."

"So, do you get extra points for creativity in magic school?" I chuckled as I pictured him using these words at Hogwarts.

His lips twitched. "Just say the fucking spell already."

Was he holding back a laugh himself? Maybe this guy had a sense of humor after all.

I said those three strange words, and the shadow-tornados homed in on the crystal and slithered their way inside it. They didn't come out the other side. They clouded the inside of the crystal.

Ok. I was a badass for doing that. "Now what?"

"Now just wait."

I squinted my eyes at him. Just like a child with a new toy, I wanted to play with it immediately. I rubbed the smooth surface of the clouded mineral between my thumb and index finger and wondered how this man knew so much. Then I set it back down on the table.

The server, a twenty-something-year-old woman with short, dark hair and a fair complexion, came out of the restaurant and asked us if we wanted something to eat. I was starving, as usual, and placed an order of sancocho, and so did Damian.

"Now," Damian mouthed.

I reached for the crystal and stared at it. Nothing happened. When I looked up, the waitress was glowing an unearthly purple. Her ears were slightly pointed, her hair had a bluish-purple tint and her eyes glowed violet.

"Gracias, Milly," Damian told her.

The waitress gave a quick wink and walked back inside.

"What in the world was that?" I asked, dumbfounded.

Chapter 33

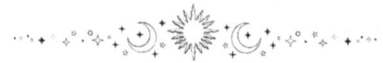

"Oh, that's just Milly," Damian answered. "She's half human, half Fae. You can only see her in her true form when you hold the crystal. Her father's the human who owns the restaurant. Her mother ran off when she was very little. The Fae don't like crossbreeds and never would've accepted her. Her mother left as soon as she was born and went back to her hidden realm.

"Her father still doesn't know her mother was Fae, but he knows something's up. Milly never did well in school. She could never grasp academics like the rest of the kids. Also, despite the glamour that keeps humans from seeing the supernaturals in this world, he's seen her do some strange things. Levitate her toys as a baby and read his thoughts, for examples," he explained casually, as though nothing about all of this was strange.

"You now have the gift of seeing the unseen with your crystal. Go ahead, take it home with you. This crystal will allow you to practice harnessing the Shadows, which is the source of your power." He frowned and leaned forward in his chair, placing his elbows on the table. "I must warn you. The dark will continue to tempt you. The Houses in Zol Stria each have their own agendas for power and control. The ruling houses were established centuries ago, and there are many who challenge them. Personally, I can't stand the politics."

I stared off into the distance and watched as a stocky, short man pushed a cart down the street. Still holding the crystal, I squinted my eyes in disbelief as his skin appeared rough and green. He possessed an extremely pointed chin and elongated ears. I shook my head and let go of the crystal, placing it back on the table.

The waitress brought out our sancocho with a side of tostones. Now that I'd released the crystal, Milly had returned to her human form.

The smell of the chicken, vegetables and spices filled my senses, and I loved the savory taste of sancocho that filled my mouth with each spoonful. After we ate, I asked Damian many more questions, and he willingly answered all of them.

"The Decree does not make shifting easy. It is a right reserved for only a select few Master Nagual. You've gotten this far," he said, never lifting his gaze from his bowl. "But trust me, it gets a lot harder."

For some reason, that didn't intimidate me at all. There was no way I was going back home anyway. My parents didn't want me, and the mafia had made it clear I couldn't go back to them. Trent was all I had, but maybe this wouldn't mean the end of us.

"Are other nagual out there right now, taking the same tests?" I asked.

"Yes. They're all part of the Zodiac Arcane Forces. But they don't all make it through the program. Now, if you do make it through, there are a whole lot of benefits to becoming a Master. It is an honored position among the Houses, and you will be rewarded."

He reached into his pocket and placed a clear jewel on the table. That had to be the largest diamond I'd ever seen.

"This is my second gift to you. This is a real, eight-carat diamond worth about fifty thousand dollars. This is your reward for getting this far. There is a financial reward for each trial, and the compensation gets greater. Trust me, niña, the choice is yours." He bowed his head and seemed slightly more... cooperative now.

"I don't think the Houses will be upset with my absence," he continued. "After eight hundred years of service, I was due for a break. But I'm willing to come back and guide you in your transformation, for I do see your potential to become a Master. And, well, maybe you can help me, too..."

"How?" I asked. There wasn't much left to decide at this point.

I picked up the jewel and held it gently in my palm. This was a paid position? Who knew being a wild-ass, jaguar shapeshifter working for some trippy parallel universe could actually pay me? *Shit,* my aunt Lily should have led with that.

This was a game-changer. I mean, I barely made anything in the military. It really would be nice to make real money for once. But in all my days hustling back home in Miami, I'd never even touched anything this expensive. Having something so valuable in my possession made me nervous. I looked around to see if anyone was watching and shoved the diamond inside my bra.

"Now how is this supposed to work? I mean, I have responsibilities."

My training to become a SERE. Trent. My mother. My best friend Nikki. Would I still get to live my life? I mean, was this like a side hustle or something?

"Go home, Nagual," he said. "Take your diamond. Relax. Play with the crystal I gave you. I'll show you more spells you can practice in the meantime. I still have to get back in touch with Command and let them know I am back on the grid."

Milly came back out and asked if we wanted anything. Damian asked for the check, then stared off into the distance.

"I get the feeling you don't want to speak to Command," I said.

"Never mind that. Now I need some time alone, please." He made a dismissive motion with his hand.

"Rude much?" I snorted.

He let out a huff. I remembered I had a fifty-thousand-dollar diamond in my bra and decided to let this one slide.

"How will I find you again?" I asked.

"Come to my shop. You'll find me," he said, voice cutting through the air like a steel blade.

Chapter 34

The sun lifted over the horizon as blue and pink clouds scattered the dimly lit sky. I ran around the track one last time before it was time to head in and considered, once again, the complete mindfuck delivered to me by Damian.

There was no way I would've believe him if my life hadn't already been so bizarre. But even if *most* of everything he'd said was true, there was the possibility that not all of it was true. He could be hiding something from me. Or just telling me what he wanted me to hear, for whatever reason.

Trent came over the next night and brought me a taco dinner he'd cooked in our community kitchen. After we ate, he looked at me with those crystal-blue eyes and said, "Sasha, I can't lose you. I've never been so scared. Don't you ever die again."

My heart ached for him. I'd never felt so much trust in another human being in my entire life. He was there for me whenever I needed him.

There were nineteen guys in this program and just one girl. He was seriously going against the grain by sticking by my side. The guys all hated me for out-hunting them, out-fighting them and even outsmarting them on our exercises. Everyone except for Trent, and he took a lot of shit for it. They hazed him, treated him like an outsider and ripped into him for being "soft" whenever they could.

One day when he'd come back from a morning run, he found his uniform cut into hearts and splayed all over his bed. Another day, he found roses stuffed into his boots. Then he woke up at 3:00 a.m. from the smell of women's perfume poured all over his bed and belongings. That night they'd poured men's cologne all over my stuff, too.

When I talked to Trent about it, he finally told me how they were making every day miserable. They called him pussy-whipped, and he was getting into all kinds of fights.

That was when I said, "Just tell them you're only here for the sex, ok? Tell them all you want to do is get laid. You can even treat me like shit in front of them. I know it isn't you, Bear. We can't both be outsiders." I meant it, too. "When we go on a mission, if we aren't a unit, we'll all just get ourselves killed."

"It's too late, Sasha. I can't stand them."

Once again, he'd chosen me.

I pushed my tacos aside and went over to him. I touched the side of his face and felt his sharp golden stubble prickle against my palm. He looked up into my eyes, and I could have melted into him right then and there. I slid my hands down onto his solid chest as I sat on his lap. He was an honest, sharp, gorgeous, bright light the right shade of sexy sin, and I wanted to show him how grateful I was to have him by my side throughout all of this.

His fingers slid around my waist and drew me in closer. His lips brushed against my cheek on the way to my ear, and I felt his warm breath on my flesh. It sent a pulsing tingle all the way through my body.

He stopped and said, "You are worth it, mi amor."

I melted into him, and my hand turned his face to meet my lips. I sent my tongue into his mouth, and it collided with his. His lips were firm and eager against mine, and we were locked in an electric exchange as his hands moved up and down my body. It was the only thing calming the vibrations surging through me. The warmth between my legs grew and ached almost painfully for him to touch me there.

I unbuttoned his shirt and pulled it off, revealing his chiseled chest, arms and shoulders. Everything about him was lean and firm. He helped me pull my shirt over my head, then his lips met my neck, kissing lower to my breasts. He took them each into his mouth, first the left one, then the right, and he worked his tongue around the nipple while he pinched the other one with his fingers.

The heat within me grew and stung with a fiery desire. I moaned softly as his hand lowered even further to caress me on the outside of my pants. His erection grew against my thigh until it felt like it would burst out through the fabric. My hands reached for him as his hands reached for me, and we pushed and pulled against each other until all our clothes were completely off.

He walked backward toward the bed, tugging me along, and sat down with me in front of him. My pussy still thrummed with need for his touch, his mouth on my breast and his hands gripping my ass.

He pulled his face back for a moment to look up at me and then said those beautifully terrible words, "I love you."

I froze mid-gasp. Before I could respond, he moved his hand down onto my clit and circled it. He slowly increased the intensity of the pressure while his bronze fingers ran along my slit. I panted and moaned with an untamed hunger. He slid one finger in, and my eyes rolled back in my head.

Another finger slid into my warmth, and it did nothing to quell the desire building in my overactive sacral chakra. I itched, ached and craved the length of him inside me. These fingers were just a tease, a torturous foreplay that kept me locked in a state of arousal.

His mouth moved to my breast again, and his breath warmed my flesh as his tongue played with my nipple. He went from one to the other while his fingers continued to slide up and down inside me. His other hand squeezed my ass so tightly I was sure it would leave a mark. I wanted to tell him to stop, to shove himself inside me and fill me with his cock, but I couldn't utter one word in this state.

He slid his fingers out of me, and my body trembled from the incessant ache of desire. Goose bumps lined my entire body, and I tingled all over. My eyes locked on his massive dick, and its size, although familiar by now, still surprised me. I went to seize it, but before I could he clutched both my hands and pulled them away.

He laid me on the bed and pressed my hands down. His mouth once again met my flesh, lower and lower until he covered my slit with his tongue. He brought me to an even higher state of sensation.

"Trent," I moaned, voice cracking. "Trent..."

I called his name even louder as he brought me to a warm, wet and succulent peak with only his mouth.

I shook all over as he lifted his lips from my folds and crawled up to meet me. I could smell myself all over him, and it felt as though I was marking him as mine. He climbed onto me, pushed himself in through my warm lips. He pushed gently at first, and then I saw that fire in his eyes, the same determination I saw when we were competing in Combat Training.

He tried again and burst through the tightness between my legs to fill me up and reach all of the parts of me that needed to feel hardness. He rocked in and out while his hands pinned mine down. I wanted to reach for him, to feel his strong back muscles against my palms, but he denied me that. He lifted his lips from my neck and looked fiercely into my eyes as the force of him ground into me again and again.

As he approached his peak, I met his gaze and finally found my voice, the words a growl between moans. "I fucking love you, too."

He collapsed on top of me, and I soaked in how incredibly good it felt to have his firm and solid body resting on top of mine.

Chapter 35

It was the day before the end of the planetary Transit, and I'd been to see the shaman twice this week. He gave me more spells and taught me ways to channel the Shadows without the stone. My fire lasted for a few more seconds now, as I pulled in the familiar dark mist and converted it into a forceful energy of my own.

Damian didn't trust Colonel van Holst. He said she'd contacted him, and she was working out a way to make me some sort of double agent so I could keep my position in the military without being considered AWOL while entering the training at the Academy. But despite her sound plan, he suspected corruption. I agreed with him; I didn't trust her much either. Especially after she told me Grange would be locked up and he never was.

When I asked Damian what they thought about him going AWOL, he said no one cared. The only reason I'd found him was because I went looking. He said no one contacted him, and they'd known where he was this whole time. All he did was not recruit me, and he said that wasn't a crime. The only reasons I was interesting at all to the Academy were because I'd marked a veil jumper before I had even shifted and van Holst had notified the Zodiac Houses about me.

Veil jumpers were what they called any of the creatures of the Gates that violated the terms of the agreement between our mutual worlds. I told Damian about the zodiac dreams, the Shadows and that my Soul Contract had to be fulfilled. I told him that's how I'd learned about him. He laughed it off and told me I must have someone on the other side of the Gates looking out for me. Someone who could dream-walk.

I was to meet him tomorrow after work. The alignment wouldn't begin until midnight, so I had time to wrap things up and make my transition into the Academy. I thought long and hard about Trent every day. The thought of leaving him was tearing me apart. He had no idea about the Gates, the nagual, none of it. I didn't know how to tell him without him thinking I was crazy. But with the Colonel trying keep me in the service, I figured I didn't have much to tell him yet. At least not until I knew what the plan was. I was getting anxious, though.

I was instructed to leave everything exactly as it was. The shaman told me not to pack, not to say goodbye to anyone, not to act like today was different than any other day. But this wasn't to be at all like any other day.

Earlier this morning, we'd received orders to wear our black uniforms. We'd be headed out on a recovery mission to one of the suspected cartel camps in the mountains. There was a kidnapping last night of the family of a U.S. ambassador, and we'd received a tip they'd been taken to the camp near our location, awaiting ransom. Only five of us were assigned to the detail so we could go undetected on the back roads.

We were divided into two low-grade SUVs so we would cross unsuspectedly, and I wore my hair down and loose in the front seat to look like a local. Trent rode with me along with our CO Perez. Lazear and Mertz rode in the other car. Lazear and his crew had backed off of us since that waterboarding exercise, but he still made my skin crawl.

We arrived without incident at five in the morning at our drop point two miles away from where the captives were being held. We hid our cars in the brush and made sure we weren't followed. We hiked the rest of the way in the dark as the sun remained hidden behind the horizon. There wasn't much intel on this place, only that it was a large estate owned by the brother of a prominent politician. It looked like an expansive hacienda nestled in a valley and surrounded by farmland. The crops of choice were cocaine and opium plants.

According to satellite footage, it looked like the family was being held in the stables, but those reports were still unconfirmed. As per protocol, we broke off into teams and conducted an hour of surveillance. We reconvened and exchanged notes, careful not to talk over radio in case they picked up on our frequency. Though we had cryptic transmissions, we weren't so much worried about being understood, just worried about being detected.

The other team said they'd spotted activity at the far end of the stables, the largest part of the building. Perez directed the three of us to scale the wall and surround the stable while the others hung back to come in on our signal with one SERE covering us when we left with the five hostages. It seemed like a fail-safe plan, until everything went terribly wrong.

Trent, Miguel and I made up the entry team. As the entry officer, Trent led us in, silent and controlled.

Right before we scaled the fence, I told him, "Let's piss the rest of the team off by not getting killed on this mission."

He laughed, then narrowed his eyes. "Still too soon, Sasha."

I shrugged my shoulders and chuckled as I heaved myself up and over.

We approached the stable while it was still dark. Luckily, there were no guard dogs in this part of the yard. I really would've hated to kill a dog to keep from blowing our cover. As we got closer, I realized how big this stable was. It was more like a second house, but for horses. There were several rooms and all sorts of places where the family could be.

We peered in windows and the rooms were well furnished, clean and well kept. It looked like a country club to me. Although I didn't see any filth here, there was something else, something much worse. Shadow energy clung to the walls.

A familiar Shadow, a dark and alluring kind that commanded my senses. It lifted from the ground and swirled in a dense mist all around.

Now that I stood within the slivers of darkness, I willed the Shadows into me and called them with the sounds Damian had taught me.

"*T'ic il taak,*" I said in a low whisper, so low no one else could hear me. This was the spell Damian taught me to bring the dark energy in. He said I wasn't ready to use this without his supervision, but I just had to. I knew this energy. This was a predator. An enemy. My instincts were on high alert, and I knew I needed every arsenal at my disposal.

The Shadows surrounded me, connecting to my skin, pulsing and charging like little bolts of electricity that coursed all the way through me. My chest filled with their piercing torment. My mind remained focused on the present while my body was consumed, and this time, I wasn't even the slightest bit afraid. But I should have been.

I watched as Trent, just ahead of me, was peering in a window. I held my rifle, alert and searching, and that's when I saw him approach. When his eyes met mine, his lips curled upward slyly. I wanted to scream, but all that came out was a muffled protest as an invisible tightness squeezed my throat. I couldn't breathe, I couldn't move even if I'd wanted to, and my rifle slipped between my fingers.

Trent's eyes flared with fury as he and Miguel fired at my old TI, Michael Grange, but the bullets met an invisible shield and fell to the ground.

Chapter 36

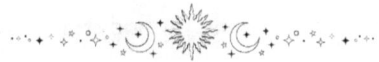

With a slight gesture, Grange did some crazy magic shit and flung the weapons out of Trent and Miguel's hands and onto the floor.

"Looks like we have visitors." Grange glanced at them in satisfaction, then returned his attention to me.

He stared at me as I continued to choke, on my knees with my arms flung behind me. I must've looked like a complete fool with my mouth hanging open like that and my eyes bugging out of my sockets.

"Now you boys come with me, or I'll strangle this one to death. It would be a shame since I was looking forward to tasting her warm blood again."

My face turned red. The lack of air to my brain prevented me from using my fire or channeling the Shadows in any way.

Trent and Miguel resentfully turned to follow him, Trent scowling with bolts of black shooting from his energy centers. As they moved to go, Grange released his grip enough for me to take two deep breaths, then locked in on me again. He pushed us inside a large room elegantly decorated with sleek mahogany furniture and terra-cotta finishes. As we entered, we discovered Lazear and Mertz on one of the couches, their eyes bulging out of their heads as they sat locked in place, a woman holding her palms open in front of them.

The woman had long, thick red hair down to her waist. She wore black leather pants, knee-high boots with a heel and a white halter top with a plunging neckline. Her fangs were completely out of her mouth, and her eyes were a bright emerald green.

Grange motioned for Trent and Miguel to join the others on the couch. Trent protested, and Grange squeezed my neck tighter. My hands were released from his brujeria, and I instantly put them around my neck and collapsed on the floor. I saw black spots in front of my eyes and felt my consciousness slipping. Trent forced himself onto the couch, and Grange released his grip on my lungs.

"I'm still not sure what you are, Beauty Queen, but I'm going to find out. Now let's handle this like adults." He came to stand before me.

My insides ignited the closer he came, my body ready to betray me in an instant. I wanted to grab him, pull him toward me and feel his hands all over my body. My neck throbbed where he'd once bit me, and it ached for him to do it again.

But I refused to give in to those impulses. Damian had warned me that the creatures of the Gates could cast their own encantos, and I'd need to learn my own counter spells before they got to me. Well, they got to me.

"I thought you weren't allowed back here." The words fumbled out with the tiniest bit of breath in my lungs.

Grange stepped toward me, and he seemed even taller now than he'd ever been before. His shoulders were broader, and there was an even more powerful allure to his deep, dark eyes.

"Endearing, really." His fingers grazed my jaw, and my arms remained locked at my sides, unable to move. "The Houses don't give a fuck about me. I'm one of the good guys. All you did was alert them to who you were by trying to take me down, and now I've found you. Back in the dorms, when I bit you, I put venom in you that marked you as my source for feeding. I can track you anywhere. And it brought me here, to this beautiful country.

"The cartel welcomed me with open arms once I took down their competition, and I've been here mastering my spells ever since. We did, in fact, kidnap that nice American family. But this morning, we'll release them of our own accord, and you six will go missing in a freak accident over one of the ridges."

"But Colonel van Holst said you would be..."

I don't know why I tried to explain anything to this monster.

He squeezed my lungs again so tightly I could barely gasp for air. Then he released me only to tilt my neck to the side and stab his fangs deep into my flesh, sending my thick, warm blood into his mouth.

The part of this that I hated the most was how much I enjoyed it. It was like I craved his skin on my skin, his lips on my neck, and his body next to mine.

When he was done, I fell into him. I reached one hand to his waist, and the other gripped his hard bicep to steady myself. I looked up into his eyes. Unable to resist, my lips parted and my chin lifted, opening myself up to him.

His deep, dark god-like eyes locked with mine, and a fire ignited within them. I pulled back, but he moved his hand to grasp my back and the other was on my waist. He bent down to kiss me—a long, hard, demanding kiss. His sharp teeth grazed my tongue and lips, and it shot a pointy pain through me. His hand reached up to the back of my head, and he pulled my hair possessively.

"I told you, I own you."

How the hell did he get so powerful? He released me from his grip, and I had to have more of him. My hands fisted his black, button-down shirt, and I clung to him. His fingers glided along my face and rested on my neck. The charge of our connection surged through me once again.

I didn't care where I was, who I was or what I was doing there. All I wanted was him. He turned me around and pressed me against the wall.

"If I'm being honest, I find it hard to resist you, too," he whispered with heated breath on my neck, making my skin thrum with desire. "I should've killed you already."

He slid his fingers down between my breasts and around my back. He gripped my ass tightly. "But the way you taste..." His voice trailed off and he pierced my skin a second time with his fangs.

My blood heated under the sting of his teeth, concentrating between my legs. Any thoughts were swallowed by the darkness invading my mind. He took another long pull of my blood. A low moan left my mouth as the heat of our embrace coursed through me.

"Sasha, no." Trent's voice was far away. My mind was so fuzzy. So hazy. But I heard him, somewhere distant.

I pushed back on Grange's chest half-heartedly, not really wanting him to stop. But then I remembered Trent. He called me again.

Wait. Just wait. This guy is a monster. What is wrong with you? I heard the tiniest voice whisper these thoughts as I fought to pull myself away from him.

"Beauty Queen, you pulled the Shadows into you." His voice held a tinge of amusement. "I can taste it in your blood. But you have no idea what you're doing." He laughed in the way only a man in complete control of his chaos could do.

I hadn't looked over at Trent until that very moment, and I never could have imagined seeing that much pain consume a person. *He is the one you love.*

Trent looked at me in disgust, in disbelief, and fiery shots of black and red left his center at an intensity I'd never seen within him before. His hands were fists at his sides, his jaw clenched.

"How... could you?" he demanded.

The others were staring at me, equally confused.

"It's not what you think, Trent! I promise, he... He has control over me."

It was too hard to explain now. He couldn't understand any of this. If it was the first time I'd seen any of it, I wouldn't believe me, either.

"Please believe me, Bear," was all I could say before Grange hovered over me once again, tightening his grip over my lungs and luring me in with his presence.

"You, I'm still not done with you." His hand on my waist gripped tighter. "We're going to one of these rooms, and I'll have the pleasure finishing what I started back at boot camp. Consider this payback for sneaking that recorder into my office." He sneered at Trent. "I knew it was you, Trent Baine, so I'll leave the rest of you for Solana. She has a pretty wild imagination."

His lips curled up into a wicked smile, as did hers.

"I've been craving a man in uniform, and now I have four of you all to myself," she said, waving her hands over them and biting her bottom lip.

They eased back in their seats, their expressions shifting from shock to lust in seconds. I wondered what she was going to do with them. Four guys, at once?

She read my mind. "Your friends will probably enjoy this more than you think, Sasha. You really should try it sometime. Four is the perfect number."

She giggled and sat on Lazear's lap. His hands went straight for her breasts, and she smacked them away. "Ah, not so fast. This is on my terms." She grabbed his hand to make him stand up. "You guys come with me. Let's give the threesome some privacy."

They left the room willingly, playful smiles on their faces and little shoves exchanged between them as they walked down a long hallway to the rear of the stable.

I shifted my focus back to Trent.

He was brooding, anger burning within and around him, and Grange was soaking it all up. Trent's energy grew and revolted, a fiery black-and-red raging cloud of energy forming at his center. Was it enough to break through Grange's spell?

Trent charged at him like the Aries ram, taking Grange by surprise and knocking him off balance.

That brief release from Grange's hold on me was all I needed to soak in every bit of darkness from the room and channel it inward. Grange regained control of his power and threw him back on the coffee table, shattering it to pieces and immobilizing Trent. He was still very much conscious, but he couldn't move.

I, however, had filled myself with so many shadows I didn't know what to do. They were taking over my senses and filling every crevice of my body with the howling plague of the shadow energy. It flooded me with so much power I had no way to channel it and no way to release it. It pressed painfully against my skin from the inside out, as if I would explode in an instant or combust. I was so lost I didn't know what the fuck I was doing.

I tried to remember the spells Damian had taught me or grab on to anything that could help me control this swirling dominion of darkness, but it was futile. My mind had spun out of control, and nothing made any sense.

The last thing I remembered was Grange's amused face as he watched me fall on all fours on the floor, gripping my head in pain as I convulsed. I imagined I looked like I was having some kind of seizure. That's when the uncontrolled beast roared out of me.

Her dark presence consumed me. She claimed control of my mind before she claimed my body and sent completely incomprehensible messages through my spine all the way to the tips of my fingers and my toes. The instructions were direct, commanding and precise, and I had no idea what they were, but I knew *she* had taken over.

Chapter 37

The Jaguar

The pain coursing through my body was the most extreme pain I'd ever felt. It was beyond words, stabbing every inch of my flesh. I heard crunching. I felt pulling, stretching and a savage ripping of my flesh and bones all at once.

The process was fast, and my clothing shredded as it fell from the deep black fur that covered my skin. I looked at my arms: they were now the front two of my four muscular, massive legs.

My mind slipped from my grasp, and I was but an echo of an observer behind the eyes of a feral beast. But I knew this beast. She'd visited my dreams and had held a calm control of the chaos around her every single time. She was calculating, decisive and free of the emotions and trauma of Sasha's world.

"Cat's come out to play," Grange sneered.

I was more than shocked to see his eyes flicker with fear.

He didn't expect this, I thought as my jaguar paced. Hell, I didn't expect this! I wasn't supposed to shift until tonight's ritual.

My jaguar turned to face Trent on the floor, and I forced a strong message into the shared mind of the jaguar: *Not him.* She turned to Grange and growled as he made several hand gestures that had no effect on us. As Grange focused his magical energy, Trent crept up from the floor and lunged at him once again, barely knocking him aside.

My jaguar seemed confused as to who the bad guy was, and she lunged at the two of them, ready to fuck them both up.

No! I yelled. *Not Trent!*

I couldn't stop what happened next.

My jaguar snarled and snapped as Trent backed away, cowering from the monster I'd become. I felt blood on the cat's paws, and blood-stained Trent's shirt from where my jaguar had scratched him.

Just then, Grange ran for the door.

Him! I yelled. *Go after him!*

My jaguar looked away from Trent and at Grange instead. I saw an unfamiliar nervous look on Grange's face. It was the first time I saw him afraid. He moved to open the door in slow, calculated movements but when he noticed my jaguar looking at him he lifted his hand as if to try some magic spell on and nothing happened. Not even a breeze. My jaguar didn't seem to like what he tried doing and she darted after him, pushing her massive paws into Trent's chest as she lifted off. He let out a groan and a cough before falling to the ground.

Its paws met Grange's back after two quick leaps over the furniture and knocked him to the ground. It pinned him to the floor and sunk its dagger-like teeth into his fragile skin. I heard the crunch and rip of his flesh and felt the blood coat my jaguar's teeth in the most delicious way. I don't think I'd ever tasted anything this satisfying. It was absolutely addicting how it filled my senses with venom, sensations and delicious flavors.

While I was absorbed in sensation overload, my jaguar didn't miss a beat as it ripped and chewed and clawed at the beast that was Grange. It took only a matter of seconds and when we turned around, Trent was holding a rifle.

It was pointed away from me, toward the hallway as if he expected Solana to come rushing through it. Keeping his position locked on the hallway, he glanced over at Grange. The TI's head, neck and upper body were a shredded mess, and the jaguar's stomach felt full and warm. She growled at Trent, still untrusting as she crouched, ready to spring.

"Sasha, if you're in there, go," Trent said. "Right now, just run before that crazy bitch comes out here."

My jaguar didn't seem to like his tone. She growled and snarled, ignoring my pleas to leave him alone.

Had I brought this on? I could feel the beast's defensive instincts. She felt threatened by him, the hairs on the back of her neck standing on edge.

Trent turned and pointed the rifle at me. At us.

This time instead of yelling, I tried to connect my thoughts to the jaguar's mind. Instead of telling my jaguar to run, I pulled on the muscles of the creature as if they were mine. Slowly, the jaguar crept backward, heeding my command.

It searched for the door, and again I pulled it toward the one I remembered walking through. It charged at the door and knocked it open with a loud crash. The jaguar must've been twice the size of any jaguar I'd ever seen and made of pure muscle.

I didn't get a chance to say goodbye or even steal one last glance at the one person in this world worth fighting for. Instead, I was carried off by this powerful creature. *Stars keep him safe.*

My jaguar ran so fast I couldn't see the trees or bushes pass by. It was just a flash. But at least I could tell the sun was coming up on the horizon, because the sky was several shades lighter. A few hundred feet in front of us was that deep purple light that matched my aura. It was much like the same light of my near-death experience. Both the cat and I were drawn toward it. We kept running, free and wild as the wind parted, and the air flowed around us.

The indigo light shone from inside a cave on the side of a rocky hill. Etched into the rocks around the entrance were ancient markings – spirals, fanged beasts and a pulsing indigo marking that seemed so familiar. My feral cat slowed to a walk and padded forward with caution. The light from the cave felt like mine somehow. The familiar glow grew brighter as we approached the boulders and rocks of the cave's entrance.

Inside the cave, I sensed another presence. My jaguar did too, and quickly scanned the dark space with its bright-emerald eyes. There at the center of the cave stood Damian. He was dressed as though he'd just walked out of a *GQ* photo shoot with a beige crew neck sweater, beige designer pants and casual black sneakers. He commanded the cave with his arms wide open, a purple-and-black mist encircling him in perpetual motion.

"*Ka nu cha'il*," he said in a deep voice that rumbled from his chest.

At once we were in the Plaza de Armas again, in Puerto Rico. A place of ancient battles, but a place a part of me trusted to be part of my legacy and now, part of my destiny.

But I realized then that this meant I was miles away from Trent. How was I supposed to help him now?

Upon the barren plaza, the sun blazed against my skin. Both the jaguar and I crouched back as we saw a massive crimson arch rise before us, flanked on either side but nothing but sky and ocean. Red, pink and black flames flickering wildly along the curved arch six hundred feet above me. The ground shifted – not physically, but energetically. From the base of the arch a bridge appeared as though summoned there by cosmic forces too grand in scale for me to comprehend. My jaguar bowed its head instinctively, as though in reverence. Like it knew that this was why I was here.

"You shifted early." The sharp edge of Damian's voice cracked through my thoughts, yanking me out of my wonder. "You must've triggered the shift by summoning the Shadows as the alignment approached. Now we have to get you to cross the Gate so you can shift back to human form, or Zol skin as we call it on the other side. This is your Aries Gate. The first time you cross must be under your constellation. You can only cross with my spells, so get your jaguar to listen and stop growling at me."

Sure, yeah. Control this monstrous beast that has a mind of its own. I was just along for the ride, asshole. My jaguar growled louder and exposed its deadly canines at Damian. There was an instinct, a knowing that my jaguar was on to him about something.

You're right! How could I have missed it?

"So, look, I know you're wondering how I found you," Damian said, backing away.

It was odd to see him so afraid. He was afraid of me! Maybe his spells wouldn't work on me in this form, just like Grange's spells didn't. Maybe that was why the nagual were chosen as the defenders. Because we were immune to the spells of the supernatural.

"I felt you. After you found me, our bond grew, and now I can sense what's going on with you. I knew you were in trouble the second he started squeezing your throat with his magic. Believe me! I'm not like him. I wouldn't hurt you. I'm here to help." His eyes were wide with fear, but his voice remained calm. "I brought you here with a teleportation spell. That's all."

He'd been through his share of confrontations in his many centuries on this planet. I expected him to be convincing, but now I wondered if we could even trust him. The Joint Celestial Command, the Zodiac Arcane Forces and the charges brought against Grange that van Holst had told me about could all be bullshit. Especially after Command let a monster like him out in the world again. I wasn't about to trust anyone, except Trent.

"Sasha, you have two clear choices in front of you." Damian's eyes raced. His words came out rushed. "Now hear me out. You either walk through this Gate with me right now so I can help you shift back into a human on the other side, or you can stay in your jaguar form forever. It's up to you—but decide quickly because you have to shift back before the end of the Transit."

My jaguar stopped snarling, the waves stopped crashing, and the wind stopped blowing. My jaguar allowed me into its visceral mind and gave me access to the intelligence within.

Chapter 38

This wasn't a mind of language. This was a mind of senses and instinct.

She smelled the fear of the shaman like she smelled the fish in the ocean that surrounded us. It was one and the same for my black jaguar, and she wanted me to sense his fear, too. His was a fear *for* me, not of me. This kind of fear was categorized differently inside its cerebral cortex. We let out a low grunt that rumbled through our chest as we worked together to process what this particular taste of fear meant to us.

I tried to communicate my understanding through the same sensory process she was sharing with me. She trusted me enough to let me in, and I wasn't about to let her down.

I tried to show the jaguar that he was afraid of what would happen to me if I was stuck inside this jaguar form forever. But my efforts were weak at best, because another part of me still didn't trust this shaman that had abandoned me and put me in this predicament by not being around in the first place. Especially after van Holst had promised Grange wouldn't be allowed back on this side of the Gates.

I couldn't trust anyone now.

I wouldn't have been able to move past this if I didn't see him how my jaguar saw him, protective and unthreatening as he stood there with his arms open and a look of desperation on his face. And of course, there was future-Sasha, who'd told me I had to go with him to the other side.

If I couldn't trust anyone else, that meant I had to trust myself.

"Look, I'm sorry I wasn't there for you before," Damian said. "I've been dealing with my own shit, and I honestly never thought you'd make it this far. Ever since Lily died, I convinced myself I couldn't do this anymore. But when you showed up at my shop, I saw so much of her in you..."

It was as if I'd just slammed into a Mack Truck. He knew Lily!

The jaguar sensed my outrage and leaped at him, knocking him to the ground. It let out a deafening roar and bared its teeth just inches away from his face.

"Yes, I knew Lily," Damian cried. He pulled his face away from my jaguar's sharp teeth, his cool composure completely broken by the weight of the beast upon him. "When I went to find you, I found her. She was your Zodiac Guardian, and we fell in love. We weren't supposed to, of course. She was married, but he didn't understand her. She wasn't happy. Then her plane went down, and I still don't know who did it or why, but I knew it was intentional.

"After centuries of serving the Houses as an immortal, she was everything to me. I would've given it all up... even mortality. I've spent years trying to find the truth about her death, and so far, Colombia is the only real lead I've found"

At that moment, all I could think about was my love for Lily. Then my mind shifted to my love for Trent and how I left him. I had to get back to him somehow, to make sure he was all right and that he'd survived.

"Cross the Gate with me now, shift back into human form on the other side, and I promise, we'll figure this all out together." His eyes pleaded with me.

The wild cat wanted to rip into him, but I pulled back. A loud roar escaped her throat that shook the rocks on the surrounding clifftop. But she eased off, and the hair on the back of her head flattened. She would follow him through the Gate.

Damian stood and brushed himself off. Although he normally seemed cool and collected, my jaguar sniffed the deep depression he'd been hiding behind his cool shaman persona. My jaguar knew before I did that he was still hurt from the loss of Lily, over twelve years ago. I totally understood; I missed her in a way that brought painful tears to my eyes. I had to stop myself from feeling this rip into my soul too deeply.

We followed him to the west side of the roof. The roof stopped at the end of the massive archway, and only the expanse of ocean lay beyond. There was no visible walkway, bridge or path into this thing.

The jaguar looked up at the shaman, waiting.

"*Xe ki haaaaa,*" he said, waving his hands at the opening.

My gaze shifted from him to the ocean and back to him again. Nothing was happening. I couldn't speak in the jaguar form, but I was dying to say, "What are you waiting for?"

Finally, a door appeared within the expansive archway. Made of metal, it was engraved with scenes of war like the rest of the structure. Out of nowhere a stone walkway appeared under the open gateway, and a man waited for us in an ornate coat of armor.

It wasn't like those bulky metal ones in those historical movies, but sleeker than any I'd ever seen. Made from a black, shiny material, it was embossed with ancient symbols of Ares, the God of War. The man was massive, muscular, his skin ebony and his features sharp and intimidating.

He studied us briefly before waving his hand over Damian's heart center, scanning him. He did the same to me, then stood aside and let us in.

Keep reading for a preview to Book II, Zodiac Chaos.

Afterword

Oh hey. It's me, Sasha.

I've taken over R.C. Luna's Afterword because she won't tell you this, but I will. She needs your review to get the word out on her books. So, if you enjoyed this book and want to help more people find out about it, show her some love by leaving a review on Amazon, Shopify, TikTok Shop, Bookbub, and/or GoodReads. It makes the world of difference.

Join her newsletter at www.rcluna.com to get regular updates on her books.

Now I gotta go. There's a whole hell of a lot more shit I'm about to get into. You have no idea. This was just the beginning.

Xoxo, *Sasha*

Sasha learns to harnesses the darkness that haunted her...

Read a sneak peak of the next book in this captivating series...

Zodiac Chaos Preview

Sasha

Now in the body of a huge and deadly black jaguar, I tried to glance behind me, but I couldn't make the thing move its head. A few seconds later, the creature slowly looked back at the large iron gate adorned with battle scenes. We had just entered the massive enclosure and a whole new realm. The gate clanked shut. Two soldiers dressed in all-black tactical gear, each with two swords strapped to his back, stood on either side.

The ruggedly handsome shaman that abandoned me my entire life, Damian, and my jaguar walked along a stone path surrounded by a lush landscape of mountains, hills, and valleys. Everything looked and seemed a lot like the places I was familiar with. Some of the mountains had snow on their peaks, and large, magnificent homes dotted the various mountainsides. The sun was just as bright as it'd been on the other side of the Aries Gate, and the shape and forms of the clouds were entirely the same, too. Yet, something was off. We were walking where the ocean was. And when the jaguar glanced back at the gate, I saw ocean where the land was. *Are land and ocean reversed here?*

The path led us through a village, and Damian expertly navigated the passageways as if he'd done it a million times. People went about their day all around us, and several of them stole glances our way. They were looking not at me, as I knew myself, but instead at an oversized feline prowling next to a tall, ruggedly handsome man. From what I gathered, the people here were into fashion and trends. They had on chic, modern clothing, which felt familiar, but there was something distinctly unearthly about the entire place. People dined at cafés, and a group of teenagers laughed by a fountain. All of this appeared normal, but the energy here was strange in a euphoric kind of way.

Is everyone glowing?

My jaguar took a deep breath and when the fresh air filled her lungs, at once I felt positive, powerful, and my mind was clear of brain chatter.

"This is a border town," Damian said with a quick look over his shoulder. It was beautiful. Everything was so fucking beautiful. "Because we're so close to the Gates, these towns tend to be the most like Earth." He pulled a key from his pocket, opened a garden gate, and gestured me inside. "The Planetary Transit will close tonight, and it takes me a while to work up the transformation spells. Just settle in, and we'll get to it."

I followed him into a large garden just inside the doorway. The center had no roof, just like the ancient Roman designs I'd seen in travel blogs. An arrangement of lush plants and flowers thrived within the square-shaped center. The garden was surrounded by a covered walkway, and Damian moved at a fast pace under covered halls until he reached an expansive room. Inside was a large wooden table lined with glasses, bowls, tools, and various bottles filled with herbs along with some modern technology and appliances.

He shut the door behind us and I felt my jaguar tense and then what felt like claws raked against her insides. My jaguar snarled sharply. He better not be setting me up. I was trusting this scum bag who had a shitty record of owning up to his responsibilities, who avoided me for almost two decades and who kept important details of my life a secret until the very last moment. *Why was I trusting him again?* Oh, right because I had no other choice.

The process to prepare the herbs took well over two hours. After pacing about for a while, my jaguar sat down at the far corner of the room, where she could watch the door and his every move as he shuffled about at the wooden work table. There was a large stone mortar and pestle in the center of the table, where he placed seeds he fetched from bottles on the shelves and then began to ground them.

Meticulously he worked, his back straight and his eyes focused, while his hands expressed the art behind this craft of spell making. They glided in the air to a methodological rhythm and swept in sequence as they reached for fresh water from the faucet, that he then poured into a carved wooden mixing bowl and added the grounded seeds. Those masterful hands pulled dried flowers from the windowsill and ground them as well, then added them with measured precision to the fresh water.

I heard him curse as he looked in every drawer for something he couldn't find, until he found it and chuckled to himself. He whispered incantations and selected more bottles from shelves, adding them to a separate glass jar he had brought to a boil with the wave of his hand. My jaguar's eyes felt heavy, and she laid her chin on the cool stone floor. I heard water running from the sink again and her eyes opened in slits. He was washing his hands in the sink, then he patted them dry on a towel, and turned to face me.

"I've got to go and get some supplies we're missing..." His now familiar thick Spanish accent snapped me into the moment and I moved to stand up. He raised his palm toward me as if he was telling me to stay like a dog. My jaguar hated that; she lifted her head and snarled at him. "I'll be right back. Please, don't leave this room." His lips curled upward awkwardly. *He better come back*. My jaguar snarled one more time before he closed the door behind him. It was infuriating being here, unable to rush back to help Trent. Powerless to save him from the fangs of a vampire.

Well now what? Aromatic herbal smells filled my senses. My stomach growled and it was as if I growled in both bodies. It seemed my human mind and my jaguar body were both hungry at the same time. I pushed the thought of eating aside. How could I think of food when Trent was in such danger?

My jaguar seemed to have her own agenda here. Her heartbeat was slower than it had been since we'd shifted, but she still paced the room that really wasn't designed for a wild animal her size. Using her teeth, she opened the door to the garden and set out to prowl the grounds. There were several rooms and stations set up just like the one we'd been in.

In one room, two men that looked like twins, both with hair like a silver fox and round glasses bent over astrological charts on a large table. They glanced up briefly, then went back to whatever they were doing without a word. In another room there was a person in a floor length white robe with the zodiac wheel embroidered beautifully in gold on the back. The white robed person was speaking to a tall, blond woman in a form-fitting, floor-length blue dress. There was a jaguar like mine curled up and napping in the corner. My jaguar turned away and padded along the corridor.

If I were to take a guess of what this place was, I'd say it was the shaman version of one of those shared office spaces like WeWork. My jaguar found another doorway that led out to another green garden, though this one seemed to go on for a few acres and was surrounded by a canopy of trees and colorful plants. After stepping out onto the grass she retreated quickly under the covered walkway, and I sensed she wasn't fond of the bright sun and preferred the veil of night.

She continued to peruse the campus and found a massive three-story library stacked with books. I immediately wanted to jump out of the jaguar's body and get my hands on some of them. What kind of books did they read here?

It felt like a long time had passed by now, and I became anxious about going back to see if Damian had returned. My jaguar must've felt it because a low growl rumbled in her chest.

Interesting, I thought.

We were definitely able to communicate with each other through our emotions. She turned and padded quickly back to the room where the shaman had left us. As soon as we saw Damian already in there, we quickened our pace to stand at his side and watch what he was doing. My jaguar's body was so large that her head met the level of the table and she could watch his every movement. His hands worked quickly, and when he was done mixing and blending, he grabbed a drink from the fridge and took a seat in a large leather chair.

"Carly, my apprentice, will be here with some food for us soon," he offered. "I need to retrieve the final ingredients from the botanist and so I'll be going out again." He seemed distant as he stared out of the large window behind the table.

His gaze turned back to my jaguar for the first time since I'd returned. It seemed a hint of fear of this beast still lingered in his eyes. Or maybe it was just respect for the wild, massive beast seated at his side.

Whatever it was, my jaguar had sensed it. Again, I wondered what powers she held. I could feel them charge through her blood. It was a constant rush surging through her veins, and I was beginning to understand that there was much more to being a nagual. It wasn't just about being a strong animal. It was about what she was capable of.

I have so much to learn.

"At precisely eleven twenty-one tonight, we will go outside on the grassy field, and you'll take the herbs that will complete the transformation." Damian arched a brow. "Once we complete the ritual, you'll be able to shift between the jaguar and human forms more freely. You'll still need to learn the process, of course, but I'll teach you. For now, just rest and relax. You're safe here."

Of course, my mind couldn't relax. What had happened to Trent? But my jaguar tuned me out completely. She had a mind of her own. When food and water came, she ate. When she was done, she slept, and when it was time for the ritual, she would go.

Damian

Here I was again, stocking up on supplies for yet another transformation ritual. How many of these had I done over the centuries? Felt like a thousand. But who was keeping track? *Twenty-One.* This was my twenty first ritual.

These humans had it all wrong. They gave up their simple, mortal lives to become supernatural beasts. Immortality was overrated. After Lily died, I made a vow over her dead body never to do this again. I never wanted to look at the face of another jaguar shifter. I thought I was done with this. It worked for one of my colleagues. He abandoned his last case before the ritual and dropped off the grid. I saw him every once in a while, socializing at the clubs in Aquarius Gate, and no one even blinked an eye at him. There was always another younger, naïve shaman wanting to climb up the ranks and impress the great Zodiac Houses with the metahumans they found as they scoured the Celestial Database for potential matches.

The only reason I came out of retirement was because Sasha found me, not the other way around. And the second I send her to Aries Academy, I'm going to disappear again. She didn't need me. She came this far on her own. Her presence unsettled me. She reminded me of Lily and I didn't want any more reminders. The only thing I wanted was to find whoever was responsible for killing Lily and making them pay over, and over. If they weren't immortal, I would use arcane magic to make them immortal just so I could torture them longer.

My feet carried me along cobblestone streets downtown, after centuries of these walks they knew exactly how to get home. Colonial Italian buildings that never changed guided my way. The walk brought me to the end of the street, where I made a right. This was the way to Ixia's, the Celestial botanist who happened to be my mentor centuries ago, during my initiation to the world of shamanism. When I arrived, I could tell she was there because the vines that lined the ornate metal gate at the entrance to her grotto were alive with purple, gold, and white flowers in full bloom. The vines detected my familiar presence and opened the Gate.

"Ixia," I grunted her name from the entrance.

She appeared before me after a few moments, while the dryads that worked with her continued toiling away at the vast herb garden. They were mostly all dressed in off white and brown dresses with plunging necklines and knee-high beige boots. Every time I walked in here, I felt the beginnings of an erection climb to the surface. Down boy! Focus on the one thing you came here for.

"You look well. Stars write the path." She cascaded her eyes up and down my body as she said this. "I heard you brought the nagual back with you. I thought you left her to choice."

"Stars write the path," I grumbled out. As far as I knew, she wasn't aware of Lily or Lily's connection to the nagual or the people I was hunting. I wasn't about to explain now. She was a Vicar and alchemy advisor to the Zol Council. Her loyalty was to the path, and I still hadn't ruled out that the Council was involved somehow with Lily's death.

"I assume she's here for the transformation ritual tonight?" She turned and walked over to a shelf lined with small wooden crates. Each identical and filled with several bottles of herbs and liquids.

"Yes. She'll make a fierce nagual I'm sure." I took in her rich, deep brown skin that was a sharp contrast to the lightness of her golden eyes. Despite being centuries old, she still looked like she was in her mid-twenties. Her curly hair was soft and brushed gently down at her sides. Her arms and neck were lined with delicate gold jewelry. The jewelry was far more than just decorative, it served to ward off the energy and spells that could do her any harm. Behind her gentle, plant-loving demeanor she was a master of protection and had developed much of the botanist program at the twelve Academies ruled by the Zodiac houses.

Ixia removed one of the small crates from the shelf and handed it to me. "We packed these just this morning. Everything is fresh."

I counted five other crates on the shelf. "So, there are six shifters at tonight's ritual?"

"Now that you're back, there are seven. Even though they all told me only six nagual would be at the ceremony, I knew there would be seven so, I prepared an extra crate." She placed her hands at her sides and a hint of mirth glimmered in her eyes. "My count has never been off. The extra crate is under the shelf." She loved to be right.

"Thanks, I'll see you there tonight then." I grumbled back at her.

"Was it my fault that you left?" Her eyes lost their bright glimmer, and her face deadpanned. *She should know better than to ask me that.*

"No, Ixia. It wasn't your fault. But you did make it easier to decide," I huffed and walked out of there, carrying my box. I didn't owe her any explanations. And she didn't owe me any.

Sasha

My jaguar form was surprisingly docile, as though it had some deeper knowing that she belonged here in the shaman's atrium. When I first shifted, just a few hours ago, I felt her wild power overtake me. Yet now, her intelligence and ability to comprehend the situation was impressive. I mean, she could just rip everyone's heads off and take off running. Which I kind of wished she would do. Especially to Damian. Instead, she chose to sit by and wait for the shaman to finish preparing the herbs for the transformation ritual.

He was so slow, too. It was driving me crazy. Every time I watched him at his worktable, he was grinding some unfamiliar herb and mixing it with some unfamiliar liquid. Then he would let the bowls sit and simmer. One under heat, another at room temperature, while he ground and mixed others. I could have sworn I saw him chop up a human eye and fire it up. Gross. But of course, I couldn't ask him anything about it because I was inside this massive black jaguar that couldn't speak.

Yet inside this beast the sounds were different. I still heard the harrowing whispers and screeches of shadow that had tormented me over the past year. But this time the screeches came through clearer, less menacing, and more natural. It was like I was hearing another aspect of nature that I couldn't understand. It didn't make me crazy with fear like when I first started hearing it, and it wasn't as annoying as it was after I began to accept it. Now, it was more like a cadence to life that I merely needed to know how to interpret.

She would scratch, lick herself, go outside and relieve herself, and I was just along for the ride. I was just a bystander inside this beast as we waited for the ritual and I began to wonder what happened to Trent. Did he survive that crazy vampire bitch? Is he alive? Is he out there worried about me? How can I let him know I'm safe? Am I safe? I'm inside a jaguar! And what if the shaman can't turn me back into a human? What if something goes terribly wrong? What if Damian is setting me up? These questions got me all worked up and my jaguar snarled. It felt like she was telling me to shut up. I couldn't believe it. We were so not connecting on this.

As the jaguar sat patiently on the wooden floor, I soaked in the décor of the room. Much like the rest of the building, the walls were made of beige stone, and they were lined with wooden shelves that held tools, instruments, books, and plants. The furniture was simple but more ornate than I was used to. Yet even beyond the architecture and design, I felt something different in my bones. I was sure it was more than just being inside the form of a jaguar. There was magic here. I could feel it prickle against her fur and smell it in the richness of the air. The jaguar took another nap and when she did, I was drawn into sleep, too. I guess our brain function was connected in this one thing. When we slept, I had the wildest dream...

I was back in my human form and running wildly back across the Aries Gate. "Trent!" I called out over the expansive white roof I was standing on. "Trent!" I screamed in desperation. I fell to my knees and cried fiercely for him. I couldn't teleport and I had no idea how to get back to him. That was when I remembered my meditation. I moved into a seated position in the middle of the terracotta roof surrounded by ocean and worked to calm my mind and focus.

I opened my eyes and gazed upon my familiar human limbs once again, on the massive pillow in Villalba, Puerto Rico. I wasn't sure how the magic worked exactly, but I knew that if I shifted into my jaguar form and looked at my reflection in the lake, I could find Trent. I ran down the soft mulch covered path under the moonlit sky to begin. I peered over the edge and saw my reflection. Then I focused on Trent's energy. Was he alive? Would I be able to find him? My heart thudded in my chest as I fought to calm panic from rising.

As much as I tried to find his energy, I couldn't. I tried again. And again, and nothing came through. Finally, I decided to seek out the dark energy of Grange even though he was dead, maybe I could . All the while I searched, it was like I was searching for a single strand of hope in a massive tapestry of darkness. Until I felt a familiar darkness, one that I had experienced before. It wasn't Grange, I couldn't find him. I assumed it was because he was dead. *Because I ripped him apart.* But I was on to the dark scented magic of the female vampire with flowing dark red hair that had accompanied him. Solana.

She was still in Colombia, still in the house where I left Trent and still had the five of my squad captured. That bitch! *Did she drain them all?* Blood dripped from her mouth as she sat on the bed with their bodies lying motionless all around her. She seemed to have had quite the time with them. Her pick of any to feast on. *Are they even alive?* That's when I spotted Trent, sprawled on a couch across from where Solana sat on the bed. I focused in on him, his energy was very low but that was normal when people slept. Their auras weren't nearly as bright. I let out a shallow breath when I saw that he had a dim aura.

He was alive!

I watched for a while, soaking in as much as I could of his face. Not sure when I would see him again.

After a couple of minutes, she sat up and that vampire bitch Solana pulled a cell phone from her pocket. She answered a call, "Yes the stars have taken Grange." She let out an exasperated breath. "I know. I know. But listen, I need you to get over here, now. There is some garbage to take out." She fixed her hair in the mirror, minimizing the collateral damage she had created. The death of my team, my fellow soldiers. My throat constricted and my rage fought to come to the surface. I shifted my attention to Trent.

Trent began to stir and he opened his hooded eyes. He made an attempt to sit upright. She was next to the four men from my unit that appeared to be resting, their naked bodies unmoving and covered with blood. *She's the fucking garbage. Not them.* Solana eyed Trent thoughtfully. She was practically glowing with all of that fresh blood she had taken.

"You're that little black cat's boyfriend, aren't you?" she hissed, as her eyes landed on him. Trent just stared back at her. He knew better than to give up any intel.

"I think I'll keep you all for myself." She walked over to him. He reached his hands up and around her waist as though he knew her. She lowered herself onto his lap in a slow, snakelike movement. His broad arms and shoulders encased her slim frame. She moved her head to the side and swept her long hair across her back, lightly gracing his defined biceps as his arms now reached slowly up her shirt. He seemed to be enjoying the caress and the feel of her body against his. I clenched my teeth as I saw desire for her in his eyes. Those eyes that only hours before, sought me to satisfy him. She had him under her spell. My nails dug into my palms as I watched them. It must be the same kind of spell that entranced me to Grange and had me in a fit of lust for him.

The fire began to burn deep in my root chakra spiraling up into my core. I felt the heat of it, spinning and swirling inside me with no form of release. I wanted to scream out, to yell, to make her stop and rip the flesh from her neck just like I had to Grange. I couldn't do any of it though, I was a formless nothing peering into an imaginary lake somewhere in back of the mind of a jaguar. Fuck my life.

Read more in the...
Warrior Shifter Series

ABOUT THE AUTHOR

R.C. Luna is a Puerto Rican storyteller who believes that the magic of stardust binds us by invisible threads of magic and destiny.

A lover of fantasy, mythology, and the supernatural, she creates immersive worlds where passion collides with power and the line between light and darkness blurs. She grew up in South Florida, surrounded by a vibrant fusion of cultures and beliefs that inspire her work. Her time in the U.S. Air Force and her travels through Latin America deepened her fascination with folklore, mysticism, and the echoes of ancient civilizations. When she's not writing, she dives into fantasy romance novels, gazes at the moon with a cup of coffee, or brings to life stories where love is as dangerous as it is irresistible.

Sign up for her newsletter for updates on new releases, exclusive lore, events and so much more!

www.rcluna.com

Looking for trouble?

You just found it. Here's where the magic gets messier — follow me and subscribe below for all the juicy updates.

www.rcluna.com

TikTok @author_rcluna

Facebook @authorrcluna

Instagram @author_rcluna

Acknowledgments

There are so many people I want to acknowledge on this writing journey. I wouldn't be here without them, and I'm deeply grateful for their love and support.

First — **thank you** to *you*, the reader. For picking up my books, leaving reviews, sharing your thoughts, and letting these characters live in your mind for a while. Creating this series would have been impossible without the support of this beautiful book community and everything you see in these stories.

At the very top of my gratitude list is my husband, Manuel. Without him, I wouldn't have written a single word. He's the one who tells me to keep going when I want to give up. Writing is my soul's passion. It's nothing but love for the craft — and time is the gift that brings it to life. Manuel gives me that gift again and again, holding it down with the kids, the house, and all the chaos life throws our way. When distractions pile up, he's the one who sends me back to my world — to let my imagination run wild and bring new ones to life. Of course, my three daughters are my fiercest cheerleaders. Their encouragement lights me up every step of the way.

I've also been blessed by an incredible circle of authors who share ideas, offer guidance, and read my work with open hearts. Their feedback and support have meant everything.

To my amazing editor, Shavonne Clark — thank you for taking these books to new heights with your expertise. To my ride-or-die beta readers, Nola and Jessica — you've been with me for every single book, and your insight has guided my growth more than you know. To Kristen, who may never truly understand how deeply her help shaped the creation of this series. And to Erika, whose thoughtful and generous guidance brought new life to this second edition. I wouldn't be where I am without the amazing book community that has found my books, and given me the motivation to get this far!

And of course — my dog, **Rumi.** Whenever I needed a hug, he was always there.

If I left anyone out, I'm truly sorry — and deeply grateful for you, too.

www.ingramcontent.com/pod-product-compliance
Lightning Source LLC
LaVergne TN
LVHW041810060526
838201LV00046B/1200